THE MADDY SAGA

BOOK TWO

THE TRAINING OF A PONYGIRL

BY

I0525733

PAUL BLADES

Cover Art by Agnes Knox
agnesknox@simonas.se
agnes.knox@gmail.com

Dark Visions Publications
darkvisionspub@gmail.com

All characters and events portrayed in this work are
fictitious

Previously published:

Watch for publication of the other books in the Maddy Saga:

Other books by Paul Blades:

Klitzman's Isle
Klitzman's Empire
Klitzman's Paradise
Klitzman's Pawn Part One
Klitzman's Pawn Part Two
The Taking of Cheryl Part One
The Taking of Cheryl Part Two: Slaver's Bait
Comfort Girl No. 4
Sacrifice to the Emerald God
The Blue Cantina: Anna's Surrender

CHAPTER ONE

In the basement of the whorehouse known as "La Papaya", literally referring to the succulent tropical fruit, but colloquially translated as "the slit" or "the pussy", a young, heavyset, naked, pale skinned, American girl peers out from a tiny cage set in the wall. She is wearing a thick, black leather gag and her hands are bound behind her. She has little idea of where she is.

What she does know is problematic enough. She had found herself rescued from the clutches of fiendish slavers by a nice little man in wire rimmed glasses. He had called himself Irving. He and a slender but powerful man that Irving referred to as Jake, had found her locked in a cage in a dungeon like prison under a barn near a farm house located somewhere in Georgia.

Irving had explained to her that she was safe now. He had helped her shower and provided her with clothes. The girl had been treated horribly in the "hole", as it was called by her captors, and she believed that she had been abandoned to die when the man and his cruel wife's bodies had been unceremoniously dumped by unknown assailants into the hole one day. She had seen the trapdoor shut and began to believe that she would starve to death locked in her little cage well before anybody ever found her.

It was with joy that she had found herself liberated. Irving had explained to her that she could not go home quite yet because it would endanger their 'mission' to save another girl named Maddy who had passed through the Georgia farm on her way to sexual slavery. They would find a hospital or sanitarium somewhere where she could be held incommunicado until the 'mission' was completed. Irving promised that he would come to get her himself.

An ambulance had come and she was hustled off in it. She was given a shot to "calm her nerves". The next thing she remembered was that she was lying in the back of a van, naked, gagged and hooded. She surmised that she was in Mexico when she was finally removed from the van and hustled into a warehouse. The unmistakable sounds of Spanish surrounded her as her body was poked and prodded. Despite her futile protests through her gag, she was raped repeatedly and then thrown into a cell.

After about three days, the girl found herself packed in a big wooden crate and back on the road. In the next warehouse, the cells on either side of her were occupied by frightened Russian girls. The one on her left spoke a limited English, and the girl was given to understand that her two companions had thought that they were going to be smuggled into the United States to get jobs as maids.

The three girls were, after a few days, packed into small cages that were lifted on the back of yet another truck. Naked and locked in their tiny steel prisons, covered by canvas tarps, the trip took what seemed like forever. The truck bounced and jerked over pothole filled roads at an agonizing pace. The women were fed and allowed to go to the bathroom at various intervals, paying for this service with their wide open lips or their widespread thighs. On the evening of the third day, the girls' cages were unloaded from the truck and brought into the basement of the mansion in which she was now resident. The Russian girls were jammed into small cages alongside her.

* * * * * * * * * * * * * *

Irving Ostroff sat next to his boss, Jacob, or 'Jake', Barnes. Their eyes were focused on a large steel door located in the side of an industrial uniform company located in the port section of Elizabeth, New Jersey. They had been watching the door for an hour. People were on their way, nasty, cruel people. When they got there, Irving and Jake and the other members of their 'team' would have a surprise for them.

Irving was the fidgety type. He was the 'tech guy' of the outfit and he had rigged the door last night so that, once all the bad guys were in, Jake and the boys could make their move. Jake was just the opposite from Irving. He was like the half breed character you sometimes saw in Westerns, the kind that can sit and watch the horizon for hours without moving. Jake possessed that character's temperament, too. He was silent and strong. He could make people afraid of him real easy. And he was just as capable of dealing out death when he had to.

"Hey Jake," Irving asked. "How do you think Maureen's doing?"

"Who's Maureen?" Jake answered, his cool grey eyes never leaving the door.

"You know, the girl we saved back in Georgia. The one with the ambulance, you know."

Jake had wanted to leave her down in the underground prison where they found her. She was not part of their mission, and the mission was all. They had not aced the old couple who had been collecting slaves for sale to the very exporters he and Irving were now watching. For some reason the man and woman had outlived their usefulness to the international gang. But Irving had insisted. He had reluctantly agreed to let the slavers they were watching take away three beautiful young girls to whatever dismal fate awaited them. But he had drawn the line at leaving

Maureen to die of hunger locked in a subterranean cell. So Jake reluctantly brought the girl out and called his employer, Michael Burnham, a wealthy industrialist and financier. Burnham arranged for an ambulance to take the girl away somewhere where she could be held incommunicado. Burnham said he would find a place to stash her a little while.

"Oh, her," Jake answered taciturnly. "She's probably ok.'

"How do you know?" Irving asked.

Jake looked at him. "Because Mr. Burnham told me so. Now let's keep our mind on the job at hand. You can collect Maureen when this is all done."

Michael Burnham, Fortune Five Hundred member, uncle of Madeline Burnham, the girl that Jake and his team were hunting for, had been pissed when Jake had called him. The last thing they needed was reporters flocking to the home of a poor southern white girl freed from nasty slavers. It would spook the guys that had kidnapped Madeline. He made a couple calls and arranged for the ambulance to pick her up. He had told the people he had hired that he didn't give a fuck what happened to the girl as long as she didn't show up on the news. Well, why waste a nice commodity like a young white girl, even if she was a little zaftig, if you could get another $10,000 or so for her in Mexico. This way, you got paid on both ends. And no girl shipped off to be a whore in Mexico would ever show up on the ten o'clock news.

* * * * * * * * * * * * * *

Three thousand miles away, on a large estate set on the western plains of Kalikastan, a former republic of the Soviet Union, a former Red Army colonel stood in the open doorway of a large, white barn, watching the teeming rain as it splattered onto the red brick path that led to the building. It was late, about 10 p.m. It had been raining all day. There was no training for the ponygirls when it rained like this. A slip in the mud, a turned ankle and for six to eight weeks all they would be good for is fucking. He had been after Grobgy, the owner of the vast estate, to build a pavilion for bad weather training for two years. It was something that the Soviet security apparatchik now turned murderous pirate had kept putting off even though he could, with his many millions in ill gotten gains, well afford it. "A whole day's training gone to waste," Drabik thought to himself. "Shit!"

Behind him in the barn were six or seven of the other trainers and handlers. They had been drinking all day. They were all drunk as Volga boatmen by now. They had been gambling, fighting and fucking and tormenting the ponygirls all day. Actually, it sounded bad, but standing in their stalls, anxiously listening to the anguished whinnies of their fellow female beasts, gave the ponies something to do. And it made them more eager to get out and train on other days, even when the weather was bad. But on days like this, when the local streams swelled and the track was a huge circular pond, well, there was nothing that could be done.

The trainers had one of the ponygirls out now. She was a broad shouldered blonde, used mostly as part of a nine pony team. She had little grace and no speed. But she was, if you'll forgive the expression, strong as a horse. She was naked but for her leather accouterments and her soft, stretchy hood. All of the ponygirls wore, like the blonde pony did now, dark blue, stretchy, Neoprene hoods that covered the head down to the steel collars around their necks. The hood had an opening for the nostrils for air when the pony was gagged and so that the large gleaming gold ring that pierced the septum could be exposed. The opening for the mouth was large enough so that the pony's lips were bared. The blonde had a leather bridle around her head holding a thick leather bit in her mouth. When not wearing a bridle and bit, the ponies wore a mask that encapsulated their jaw and the bottom half of their faces. Inside their mouths would be a thick leather gag attached to the inside of the mask. There were tiny dime sized holes for the eyes that permitted limited sight.

The hood served as a tight, form fitting covering for the ponygirl's face, eliminating all signs of humanity. Around their necks they wore a thick, black, leather covered, plastic collar, higher in front than behind, so that their heads were constantly tilted upwards. Their wrists were enclosed in wide leather bracelets that were clipped to a strap that descended down the back from the collar. They also wore thick, leather, calf high, shiny, black boots. Their labial lips sported two golden rings, with golden disks hanging from them, which pierced the nether lips at the bottom, close to the perineum.

The game was simple. It was a drinking game of sorts. One of the men would serve out to the pony a shot glass full of vodka. She would be made to drink it back and then dash around the corridor that ran along the inside of the exterior walls of the large barn three times. When she came back, she would be served another shot, et cetera. The point of the game was to bet on how many shots she could drink before she got too drunk to proceed. And it was no use for the former young woman to fake it, because she would be savagely beaten each time she fell and made to resume her feet. It was only when she was literally too drunk to stand that the game was over. She would be dragged away to sleep it off in her stall.

Each time the pony drank back a shot, the men would give a big cheer. She would be slapped on the ass and made to run. The men would chant and sing as she made her three voyages around the barn interior. She would pass the stalls of her fellow ponies, who, with the stall doors closed, could hear but not see, the ponygirl make her rounds. Most of them were standing, chained to the wall, fearful that they would be next. For the game sounds fun, except that, when the pony started to lose the ability to stand, the losing betters would not give up until they were certain that she would respond no further, urging the game master to beat and whip her, cursing her forbears. The short lived fight that had broken out that day had been between the trainer of a particular pony who was being abused like a dead horse, and the man on the losing end of a bet, not willing to give up.

The name of the pony that was running now was Snowflake, a somewhat inappropriate name for such a well muscled animal. But she had pale white skin and hair so blonde that it was almost white. Like all the other ponies, the only hair left on her body was a long pony tail that emerged from the back of her hood and cascaded down her back. She had deliciously plump breasts that bobbed and weaved as she ran. Her thighs were thick, but graceful. Her stomach, which contained the tattoo of her owner's crest, the yellow, rampant wolf, was flat and taut. All of the excess fat had been run off this pony long ago. Her name, in Russian, was tattooed in blue Cyrillic letters across her upper chest.

The excitement of the small crowd of men was rising since she had just finished her tenth shot. She had fallen several times on her last go round, bumping into corner posts, tripping over her own feet. It would have been easier if she could have jogged slowly around the warren of pony stalls, but that would not have been in the spirit of the game. If the men thought that a pony was lagging, she would be subject to severe discipline. And it was not something that would be soon forgotten. Snowflake and the other ponies saw the trainers, and were subject to their whips, every day.

Snowflake once had a different name. She had once been a young German girl. She had had friends, lovers, a family, all the trappings of life that a normal, healthy nineteen year old woman should have. But that was almost two years ago. Snowflake now was no more a woman than a cow or a sheep. She was no longer the promising, happy nursing student that she had been when she had been taken that foggy Hamburg night two years ago. Physiologically, she was a human female. She had all the attributes. And she did retain the power to think and, technically, the power to speak. But it had been so long that either of these skills were called for that they had practically withered away. She was now a mere beast, a highly trained chattel.

When Snowflake had finished her third turn around the barn, she stood huffing and puffing in the circle of men. Each time, after forcing the shot of vodka down her throat, her bit was reapplied. It wouldn't do to tempt a pretty pony into speaking. And if she tossed her lunch because of too much booze and too much motion, at least she wouldn't aspirate it.

The game was getting interesting and the men were all excited. Snowflake's record (careful note was taken of these things) was twelve shots. The bets were pooled and the men who had chosen the next two rounds were getting nervous. Only one man had bet that Snowflake would do fifteen this night.

The pony's mind was dizzy and confused. She felt her bridle loosened and another shot of hot liquor poured down her throat. She shook her head as it clouded her eyes, causing the long, white pony tail that emerged from the soft blue hood at the rear of her head to swing to and fro. This was real vodka, over 120 proof. A hand plied at her hairless pussy, trying to stimulate her into awareness.

The faceless pony's bit was replaced and she was given a solid slap on her hindquarters. Off she went, her blue clad head leaning slightly forwards, her jug-like breasts swaying beneath her, her useless hands buckled to the strap from her collar behind her back.

Remarkably, the pale white pony made it through the fourteenth round. In the last round she had fallen four times, once in the second lap and three times in the third. Her body was criss-crossed with angry red lines, denoting the encouragement that she had needed to complete her last few laps. Even the men who had lost their bets were excited. There were three men who had bet fourteen, and they were hoping that Snowflake would collapse on her next round. She could barely stand as she waited for her next shot. Some of it dribbled out of the corners of her mouth and there were angry demands that she take another. Cooler heads prevailed and the shot glass was only refilled half way. The pony's whole body seemed to sag. She had broken no speed records on her last laps, and there was no reason to believe that she would do so this time either.

After her bit was replaced, she received a sharp slap and she began to run. She was running so slow that the men were able to walk behind her as she made her circuit. The first lap she fell three times, crashing into a wall, stumbling over her own feet, clipping her shoulder on a corner post. She was barely conscious, driven only by two things: fear of the whip and a desperate need for obedience, something that had been beaten into her day in and day out for over seven hundred days.

There was a round of shouts when Snowflake completed her first circuit. As she reached the starting point, her whole body seemed to collapse. Her body struck the floor with a loud, "thump!" Not having hands to brace herself, her naked breasts and forehead took the brunt of the impact with the floor. The race master, the only one who had no bets and whose judgment was thus not biased, gave her pale white rear and legs several sharp blows with the whip. The soused pony whined and moaned as she was struck. Even through her drunken haze, she could feel the whip's sting.

It is tough enough to raise yourself to your feet with two hands when you are stupefyingly drunk, but consider how hard it is without the use of your arms. Snowflake's were bound up behind her. The muscles there had all but atrophied. But her by now nearly instinctual training pierced her drunken fog and she was able to push herself to her feet, using her strong legs. Off she trudged again. This time, her pace was reduced to almost a crawl. Some of the men protested and she was given a sharp "crack!" on her naked ass to encourage her to speed.

By the third lap, Snowflake was more weaving than running. No amount of whipping could make her go faster. One more fall would be her last. The man who had taken fifteen as his number shouted encouragement to her.

"Come, Snowflake, come!" he yelled in Russian. "Faster, faster!"

The poor pony had little volitional ability left. Her knees barely rose as she dragged one foot after the other. "Come on, Snowflake, you can do it!" the man yelled, walking next to her as she struggled to put even just one more foot forwards. She was 10' from the finish. Just before crossing the finish line, she fell to one knee. Her body wavered. She was trying desperately to move the last few inches forward. The referee had laid off the whip. The room was silent as the men watched the Herculean struggle of the naked and hooded ponygirl.

After pausing for at least twenty seconds, Snowflake dragged her back leg forward. She could not cross the finish line on her knees. That was the rule. The man who had the number fifteen was standing next to her, whispering into her ear. "One more step, lotchka, one more! You can do it! Lift your leg, raise it high!"

The former German nursing student, Louisa Schellman, now known only as Snowflake, pulled her left leg up. She raised herself to a crouch; her knee was off of the floor. She gave one last, powerful push with her right leg and she stumbled across the finish line, She fell literally flat on her face, her body making another loud "thump!" on the floor. There was a moment's silence, and the men erupted into cheers. The man who had bet fifteen shots smiled broadly as he received hearty backslaps from his drunken fellows.

Who was this man with so much faith in this powerfully built pony? It was her trainer, of course, Anton Drabik. What other voice did this pony know so well that it could pierce her benumbed senses? Who else would she produce a super human effort for?

The party had gone on long enough. Snowflake was left to lie where she had fallen. Later, one of the watchmen would drag her into her stall and chain her ankles and collar to the floor. Drabik received his winnings like a gentleman. Good winning was just as important as good losing. The betting had been heavy and Snowflake had earned him a hefty prize. But tomorrow was tomorrow, and, hung over or not, she would get a full workout.

The other men stumbled off to bunk down for the night. Drabik had a stop to make before retiring.

Maddy, the former Madeline Burnham, had listened to the raucousness of the drunken men with great anxiety. She had been a pony for only ten days, and the customs and habits of the pony barn were new to her. The day had begun like all of the rest since she had been, literally, dehumanized. She had awoken that day lying on a cotton filled pallet on the floor of her stall. A chain ran from her neck and ankles to rings in the floor and her thighs and ankles were strapped together, making any significant movement through the night impossible.

The ponies slept gagged with flaps over the eyelets to their hoods closing out all light. The flaps were built in to the hoods, with Velcro on both sides so that could be fixed open or closed. Maddy had awoken it seemed like hours earlier, but since her sight had been taken from her she didn't know whether there were gleams of morning light through the windows or whether the barn and all who were in it were still wrapped in darkness. She could hear the steady drumming of the fierce rain on the roof. It mesmerized her, made her think of other stormy nights a world away from where she was now. She had tried to steel herself against tears. She knew that absent some miracle she was going to be in the power of these evil men for a long time, maybe forever. She had to be strong! Sometimes, though, it was the little things like rainfall drumming on the roof, or the sight of the open sky, that set her off.

She sniffled as the tears insisted on coming. She mourned the fact that she could not move her legs, roll over to her stomach, scratch an itch. She could hear the faint sounds of rattling chains from the stall next to hers. She had no idea which of the ponygirls was lying there helpless and bound, would probably never know anything about any of the other hapless, former young women who had been condemned to this perverse and bizarre life. If only she could talk! She would beg for freedom, promise anything. But as misery swept through her, she realized that even if she could supplicate the cruel men who had mastery over her, it would be of no use. They would laugh and shove their conscienceless pricks into her.

Finally, she heard the sounds of the barn beginning to stir. She did not know whether it was her trainer or one of the broad shouldered, muscular, stable boys, young men really, who had loosened her chains until the flaps over her hood's eyeholes were lifted. This day it was the tall, blond haired stable boy. He helped her to her feet and then let her pee in the corner chamber pot. She looked at him forlornly. He could not see her expression. She was just a hooded, female creature. It embarrassed her to be naked in front of what was really a mere boy, someone her own age. He was handsome and his face was kindly. But he had beaten her the other day nonetheless.

The stable boy released her gag and removed her hood so that she could eat her porridge from a little bowl on the floor, on her knees, like a cat or a dog. Maddy hadn't seen her face for many days and she tried to remember what she looked like. Not even her trainer or the stable boys had viewed her facial features since her arrival at the estate. Whenever her hood was removed, they were careful to have her face turned away so that she would remain an anonymous, former person to them. There was only one part of her face that was visible when her hood was on and she was not wearing her mask. That was her plump lips, circled by the mouth opening on her hood, as they parted to receive a swollen male member or when she was wearing her bit, for, other than when she ate, her mouth was not released for any other purpose.

Maddy hadn't decided if the hoods made the ponies look comical or sinister. It was psychologically devastating to realize that your face was essentially featureless and that observers would have to depend on the bright blue letters etched across your chest to ascertain your identity, unless, of course, they recognized the shape of your breasts, or the curves of your ass.

The stable boy cleaned up her face and then performed the ritual daily shaving of her head. Maddy still could not hold back her tears as she felt the sharp razor clean away her meager growth from the day before, leaving only the long strands of her tail, the remnants of her beautiful, auburn, waist length locks. It would have been more efficient to use a depilating agent, but the daily experience of having her head shaved was just one more way of reminding the pony that every facet of her bodily functions was under the control of her masters. When Maddy's head was shaved and a creamy lotion applied, the stable boy immediately reapplied her hood and gag and then repeated the process with her loins, forcing her to lie down, spread her legs and bend her knees so that he could have easy access to her nether lips.

Usually, in the mornings, she and the other ponies were taken up to the track and given a morning run. Because of the newness of her tattoos, Maddy had stayed in the barn for the first couple of days after receiving her marks. The first day, the first full day after her arrival and before she was marked with her owner's crest and her new name, she had been led there to run without knowing what was happening. When the other ponies took off, she was literally left in the dust. Even if she had been alert, she would have finished last, not having the muscles or stamina to keep up. The routine was that the last pony to finish took five strokes from the whip. Her position, bent over a rail, was also suitable for access to her nether parts and the pony could reasonably expect to be ravished after suffering five burning blows across her hindquarters.

The second day that Maddy ran, she knew what to do, but still finished dead last by a wide margin. The men laughed and joked as they used her. They kept her bent over, her ankles fastened wide apart, the ring in her nose fixed to a ring in the ground, plowing her hot sheath until they heard and felt the signals of her orgasm. She cursed herself and the men who were raping her even as her cunt sent paroxysms of pleasure to her brain. In fact, Maddy had finished last every day that she had made the run so far. But she felt that she was getting better, stronger. Soon, she knew, she would not be last.

This was partly due to the fact that Maddy had the best, most exacting trainer on the estate, Anton Drabik. He supplemented the punishment she received at the hands of the other trainers for her poor performance. He had a four foot long leather encased reed that he used. Maddy would take ten across the breasts and thighs after she was released by the other trainers to supply added motivation to improve.

The newly collared pony, although she still foolishly thought of herself as a young woman, had determined that she would be the best ponygirl that she could be. She hated the sting of the whip and she resented the laughter and jibes that were thrown at her when she failed, even though she spoke barely a word of Russian. But she was beginning to understand some. She knew the word for "faster" and the expression for "spread your legs". There was one expression that she wasn't sure whether it meant "suck my cock" or "open your mouth". It didn't matter. The phraseology produced the desired response.

It was an important training principle that the ponies not be exposed to more actual language than necessary. They were trained instead to respond to hand signals or a pull on their reins. And their new name.

Each of the ponies wore their name emblazoned in bright blue ink across their chests. Maddy's new name was "Lightning", and the Russian word, "Molnya", was spelled out in large Cyrillic letters just above her breasts. She had seen the letters in the mirror, but she didn't know what they meant. At first, she couldn't even pronounce it. But she had learned that the expression she heard as "molnya" meant she should pay attention, and sometimes her trainer soothed and rewarded her with the sound after an especially hard workout, or an energetic fuck. When fucking her after yet another poor performance on the morning run, the men would call it out and laugh.

But this morning there had been no run. The ponies had been paraded around the barn's interior just so they could get some exercise and get out of their stalls for a little while. Right after breakfast, lunch and dinner, the stable boys or the trainers unleashed them from their bindings and led them twenty full circuits around the interior of the building.

But the rest of Maddy's day was spent with her hips leaning against a horizontal post that extended across her stall about three feet high, her legs spread and fastened wide apart, and the ring in her nose chained to a hook on the wall. Little voluntary movement was possible.

A thousand thoughts raced through Maddy's mind during the course of that day. She remembered her kidnapping and being held prisoner in a strange dungeon. She recalled her callous treatment at the slave way station, where they had shaved her head and first applied the raiment of her new life upon her body. She cried from time to time as she thought of the people she had left behind, the life that she used to have. Kidnapped on her way home from night classes at college, she went through the many "what if's" that would have spared her this fate. What if she hadn't gone to school that night? Or taken that class? What if she hadn't gotten into that van when her car so conveniently 'broke down'? What if she had agreed to let her rich Uncle Michael pay for her room and board at a prestigious private college up north?

And then pure and unadulterated anger would sweep through her. She would rage at her unkind fate, the cruelty of the men who had stolen everything from her, the men who used her body like they would a whore's, but even worse. When these fits overcame her, and they were perfectly normal for a new pony just breaking in, she would stomp her booted feet, struggle against the bonds that held her, roar behind her thick, leather, mouth covering gag.

It was after the luncheon walk that the trainers and some of the stable boys had got to drinking. Maddy heard them laughing and joking, almost obscuring the muffled moans of the ponies that they were abusing. Maddy cringed when she heard her stall door open behind her. A man leaned under the rail over which she was partly bent and released her chain from the wall. Her ankles were undone and she was led by the nose out to the common area of the barn. The men had spread a large cloth over the floor and two ponies were in the middle of it. Maddy could see the forms of their pale white, naked bodies and their melded mouths through the small holes in her hood. Their gags had been removed. They were kneeling, their chests pressed together, and were engaged in a passionate kiss, their blue, featureless, expressionless faces conjoined at the mouth. The men were seated around the ponies, laughing and joking as the ponies' mouths worked hungrily, their pretty pony breasts rubbing against each other's.

When the men saw Maddy, they gave a little cheer of approval. One of the men rolled out a wooden frame. Maddy felt her self pushed down over onto it. Her torso was bent over on top of a three foot wide, padded board. There were round cut outs in it, placed strategically so that her melon sized breasts fell right through. Her legs were spread and her ankles affixed to the bottom corners of the frame. Her head went through a little slot, and her collar was tied in place.

The finishing touch was when her gag was removed and a wide, hard rubber ring gag was forced into her mouth. Her collar kept her mouth poised at just the right angle for penetration.

Maddy struggled at her confinements, frantic at the prospect of her impending gang rape. She felt a hand fondle her hairless nether lips, running a finger between them, coaxing her pussy to lubrication. One of the men stepped in front of her and withdrew his thick, turgid cock from his pants. He grabbed the long, reddish brown colored ponytail that emerged from her face encompassing hood and presented his hardened meat to her lips. Maddy's body tensed as she prepared to receive his thrust. All she could see of him was his manhood and his denim clothed legs, a pair of rough, khaki boots. He teased her by rubbing his cock along her distended lips. She heard that word again, 'molnya', mixed in with other unintelligible sounds.

Behind her, the unknown hand that was manipulating her proffered sex, thrust its fingers deep within her. She gave an involuntary moan as her pussy welcomed the thick digits. The cock at her mouth pushed inwards, depressing her tongue. Futilely, bordering on panic, the young pony's body shook. The unknown man pushed his cock past the edge of her throat and descended within. She could feel her esophagus expand as it made way for the thick, hot meat. The man groaned with pleasure as he felt his prick enveloped.

Maddy continued to be enflamed by the relentless hand at her pussy. She was utterly helpless to prevent her passion's rise. As her head was forcibly drawn slowly up and down on the cock that cruelly pierced her mouth, the hand behind her was removed. She felt a hardness press aside her nether lips and delve between them. Hands fastened themselves on her pale, round hindquarters. As the heat of the stiff cock mingled with hers, she moaned in frustrated pleasure. The cock behind her slowly pressed on, dragging across her hardened clit, until she felt it buried inside her to the hilt.

At the same time that her pussy sent a wave of lust through her, Maddy began to struggle for air. The cock in her throat slid slowly out, until its plump, round head passed over her lips once again. She was able to inhale deeply, before the stiff pole returned and was slowly edged down her throat.

Maddy had never been fucked by two men at once before. She had heard of such things from girlfriends back in Cleveland, before she moved with her father south to

Tennessee, who had "taken on" more than one young boy at a time. They had told her how their body felt totally filled and how their minds became overwhelmed with the sensations of servicing two hard, hot cocks at once. The now lust filled pony was reminded of their tales of promiscuity as the twin staffs probed deep inside her.

The men were in no hurry. There was ample time. It was going to rain all day, and what else was there to do? They purposefully let their cocks linger in the warmth and tightness of Maddy's orifices. They could sense the building lust in her and it served as an enhancement to their own pleasure.

Maddy's body now was trembling with passion. Her dangling breasts were aching and hard as they filled with her excited blood. Her bound hands clenched in frustration behind her. She yearned to meet the thrusts of the two men, to quicken their movements, to push her over the crest of pleasure. But the men were tantalizingly slow, taking their pleasure within her at their own pace. The lust filled pony dragged her tongue along the thick, hot meat in her mouth as it slowly pierced the entrance to her throat and then just as slowly withdrew. Her mouth salivated, anxious for the salty taste of the man's discharge just as her pussy craved the splash of the hot seed of the man behind her. Suddenly, her body began to jerk and spasm as her pussy began its lustful contractions. "Gaaaaaaaaaa!" she exclaimed as the meaty tube in her mouth distorted her passionate moan. Just as her orgasm reached its peak, she felt the man behind her quicken his pace, his urgency sparked by her display of lust. As his prick began to throb and pulse within her, her contractions began anew, driving her past all rationality. "Gaaaaaaaa! Gaaaaaaa!" she called out as wave after wave of ecstasy flowed through her.

The man before her pressed his cock deeply inside her throat and groaned. His cock began to spasm as he dumped his load of hot spewm down her esophagus. The sensation of two pricks exploding within her at once drove Maddy wild. All the world seemed to pass away as her consciousness was overwhelmed by her pleasure. Never had she come so hard and for so long.

The men, having had their way with the new ponygirl, withdrew themselves from her body. Her cunt yawned, empty, and her body regretted the cessation of its sexual torment. Her heart was beating wildly within her, and she panted breathlessly.

Within a few moments, another pair of hot pricks beckoned at the doors of her body. Hard meat was again thrust into her mouth and into her sensitized pussy. Maddy groaned with completion as the cocks began to batter at her gates. These men, excited by the ardor raised in the bound and helpless pony, succumbed to their cock's needs and thrust hard and ruthlessly into her. Once more, Maddy's body shivered and convulsed as hard jolts of electrified passion shot through her. When the men jetted their slimy discharges within her, Maddy screamed,

For a while, Maddy was permitted to lie upon her little altar, to recover her senses. Slowly, she began to refocus on the world around her. Her platform was wheeled around and pointed at the two ponies who were still engaged in a passionate embrace on the barn floor. Through the tiny embrasures in her hood, Maddy could see that the lithe, young females had their faces buried in each other's quims and that their black booted feet and muscular legs were spasmodically jerking and pounding on the floor as they came. For a moment, the fillies slumped with bodily fulfillment. There was the sound of a whip and a dark, red blotch appeared on the hindquarters of the pony on top. Instantly, she buried her face anew between her partner's thighs and began to grind her pussy in the other pony's face.

Just as the two ponies recommenced their consumption of each other's lust, Maddy felt two hot hands part the rear globes of her hindquarters. A hand dipped into her sopping cunt and, drawing from her a swipe of her viscous discharge, smeared it across the tiny aperture to her bowels. She felt the head of a rigid cock presented to the tiny star and begin to force its way inside. Although lubricated, her brown lips of her rear entrance were not yet used to the stretching force of a thick, hard cock, and her delicate tissues began to tear painfully. "Ough! Ough!" she called out as the pain shot through her, her ringed mouth unable to form words. As the man plowed her rear and the burning began to subside, the sensation of his cock drawing across the tender skin of her anal ring began to send shoots of pleasure to her loins. At the same time, Maddy's mind revolted at this act of forced sodomy, which had been darkly referred to by her parents and friends as a practice of extreme depravity. She hated her body for welcoming it and she helplessly kicked her bound feet and wrenched her confined torso in a futile attempt to expel the fat, hot intruder.

The ponies on the floor in front of her had reached a new crisis. Their bodies had rolled and they had exchanged positions. Maddy watched the rear of the topmost pony grind and thrust at the mouth that tortured her loins. Her brown ponytail was splayed across her broad back, draped across her imprisoned arms. Maddy felt the hips of the man behind her press against her hindquarters and heard the man groan as he shot his load into her bowels.

Almost as one, the crowd of men seemed to lose interest in tormenting the young females. They were permitted to regain their feet and their gags were replaced. They each received a resounding slap on their behinds before being led back to their stalls.

The men began to don their rain gear and trudge from the barn. When the door to the barn was opened, Maddy, as she was being escorted back to her stall, could hear the dinner bell tolling. There was a long, wooden building that served as the trainers' bunkhouse, and the men mostly took their meals there. In an hour, they would be back to feed and walk the ponies.

Two stable boys remained as custodians of the barn full of former young women. They dutifully walked the rounds, checking each stall, ensuring that all the ponies were firmly secured. It was hard for even grown men, never mind young men in their late teens or early twenties, to peruse the volume of naked, desirable female flesh without stimulation of their carnal needs. These two boys were no different. Maddy, having been returned to her former position in her stall, the cum of three men leaking down her legs, heard the boys remove two of the ponies for their use.

After her dinner walk, during which she was led by Drabik himself, she was taken back to her stall. He washed the residue of her afternoon activities from her body. Instead of chaining her facing the wall, he forced her to lean back on a specially designed board mounted on the rail that ran across her stall about waist high. Her torso was tilted backwards and her ankles chained to the rail, her legs splayed wide. Maddy knew that this position was meant to make her lower orifices readily available for invasion. Drabik caressed her breasts and rubbed her delicate nether lips until he saw the signs of arousal on her body. Then he left to rejoin his mates, already engaged in the abuse of another female.

So it was thus mounted, ready for use that Maddy listened to the wild partying of the men, their shouts and cheers, the clip clop of the ponies' boots as they made their frantic journeys around the barn. She heard the crack of the whip, the unmistakable sound of bodies hitting the floor, the curses and swears of the men who had lost their bets. She anxiously awaited her impending use. She still reviled each unconsented to invasion of her body, and she struggled and cried in frustration at her upcoming rape.

When the men had left, after Snowflake rook her nosedive to the floor, the barn became almost deathly quiet. Then she heard the steady pace of booted male feet approaching her stall. The door swung open and her trainer entered.

Drabik took a long look at his newest charge. She shook her blue manikin like head with its leather shield across her face in a futile effort to see who had come in, but the angle of her collar kept her eyes pointed upwards to the ceiling. She was progressing nicely, he thought. It would be a while yet before she was fully inured to her fate, but he could sense her humanity slipping away from her a little more each day. She had not been permitted a single word of speech since her arrival and she remained gagged even when beaten. Tomorrow, weather permitting, he would resume her training, forcing her to run while tethered to the training wheel. The other men laughed at the name he had given her, but he was a good judge of ponygirl flesh and she had all of the attributes of a winner. She snarled in misery and frustration when she finished last in all of her morning runs so far. He could see her determinedly pushing herself when he trained her, as she ran for hours on end, stopping only when compelled to do so, or after exhausting her forces, she collapsed, straining to regain her breath.

And her responsiveness was delightful. Soon, all of her thoughts would concentrate on the physical sensations of her body. She would grow dependant on sexual release and learn to yearn for a master's touch. She would gratefully accept the proffered cocks of her betters, happy to grant them their due.

Drabik could see that Maddy's nipples had stiffened at his arrival, in anticipation of her use, and he saw a slight sign of arousal glistening between the distended lips of her sex. He advanced slowly on her, increasing her anxiety. He rubbed his hands on the inside of her widespread thighs, drawing arousal from the firm, smooth flesh. He advanced between her legs and placed his hands on her breasts. They were firm and aroused and he heard the ponygirl give out a tiny repressed sigh. He crooned her name to her, "Molnya, little Molnya," as he delicately pinched her hardened nipples. When he placed his hand on her engorged pussy lips, dipping a finger between them, her body trembled.

Maddy recognized the voice of her trainer and chief tormentor. She had been waiting for him, both dreading and wishing for his arrival. He was the only one to pay special attention to her and, she hoped, he was the most likely of all the cruel men to recognize her humanity.

The former colonel took a moment to strip himself bare. He wanted Maddy to feel the heat of his body against hers. His thick cock was already stiff. He presented it to the tiny, wrinkled hole between Maddy's hindquarters, and lodged the tip of its round head just inside. She would do the work of admitting him.

Drabik leaned over and took one of Maddy's hard teats in his mouth. He suckled at it until he heard the female groan. He switched teats and teased and pulled at it with his teeth until he felt Maddy's loins shift beneath him. He ran his hand over her taut stomach, over the bright yellow wolf etched into her smooth, lean stomach, with its raging mouth and its distended paws. Maddy's body pulled up slightly on her board, as if to frustrate her trainer's intent. But when he delved his thumb deeply into her cunt, her body welcomed it.

He caressed Maddy's pussy until it began to gush. Slowly but surely, his cock was sliding towards its goal: immersion in the pony's hot bowels. Maddy's hips began to rock and her breathing became heavy. As she was approaching her orgasm, Drabik withdrew his hand causing her to emit a groan of frustration. Her blue covered head shook pleadingly. As her body writhed, begging for the resumption of its trainer's caress, the ring of her anus began to loosen. Drabik's thick pole inched forward. Its head was now just past the tight circle of flesh. When Drabik resumed his attentions to Maddy's cunt, she moaned and, after drawing her torso and hips as high as they could go, pushed down, embedding Drabik's cock deep within her ass.

Maddy had felt the thick rod pressing for entry at her rear hole. She dreaded its invasion, but the caresses of her trainer's hand infused her mind with lust. Her body craved possession and the need to feel a hot, thick cock inside her permeated her being. She ceased to care what entry was used. She wanted to be filled and so she pushed her hips downwards driving Drabik's piece inside.

As Drabik pumped his meat across the sensitive opening of her bowels, he teased her hardened clit with his fingers. His thumb was deep inside her pussy, caressing its swollen walls. The ponygirl's hips pushed back at him wildly. He could hear her moan from deep within her throat. He took his hand from her sex and placed it on the rail. He began to rasp his manhood across the tender and electrified skin of her now distended anal ring. The only contact between their bodies was the interface of his stiff manhood and the entrance to her bowels. She would come this way or not at all. Suddenly, Maddy emitted a long, plaintive wail and then her body began to shake and convulse. Her firm, plump breasts danced upon her chest as she drove her hips hard downwards seeking to increase the friction of their embrace. As Maddy screamed and moaned, her orgasm sending convulsive spasms throughout her body, Drabik's manhood began to throb and spurt. He pumped his fluid deeply within her and groaned out his own pleasure.

Maddy's convulsions gradually eased. Her body was covered with a sheen of sweat. Her chest pumped hard, seeking to renew the oxygen driven from her blood by her wild exertions. Drabik withdrew his softening tool and stepped back. He wiped himself clean with a wet, soapy cloth, dressed, and then released Maddy from her bonds lowering her body to the cotton pallet on the floor of her stall. After confining her ankles and collar to the short chains he found there, he covered her eye holes. He gave her breasts a tender squeeze and then left.

CHAPTER TWO

Jake watched as the last of the men entered the side door to the large, yellow brick industrial building. Now that all of the targets were there, he gave Irving the nod to signal Leon and Mary Ellen to make their move. Leon had been with the crew since Georgia, but Mary Ellen he had brought in especially for this job. She was smart, efficient and deadly. And he knew for a fact that she had few moral qualms, something that would be helpful for the next stage of the plan.

It was about 3 A.M. The streets were deserted. The uniform warehouse was located in the middle of an industrial park; ideal for the purposes of the gang that ran this slaving operation. Nights and weekends, the place was almost deserted.

It had been somewhat of a problem to come up with a strategy for blowing the large steel reinforced door that faced the side street. They couldn't blow the main garage doors, because they would be too hard to replace. They had to have everything looking hunky dory by morning or the whole plan would come apart. But the problem was how to set the charges, specially designed charges made up by Irving, the technical specialist, to just blow the hinges and to do so without too much noise. Irving had developed a special canister to go over the charge that was heavily lined with fireproofed, sound deadening materials. The canister had a latch that would hook onto the door. The explosion was designed to go inwards. The canister would stay on just long enough to deaden some of the noise. It wasn't perfect, but it would have to do.

Jake had managed to get good pictures of the door opening and closing, and the heavy bolts that held the door closed when it was locked would have required strong explosives to blow. They would have taken off all the brick surrounding the point of impact. He had also gotten good shots of the interior hinges. The explosion Irving had designed would pierce the steel door and shatter the steel hinges. The door could then be pushed open.

But there was another door inside. It was a large garage style door. They would have to blow that too. They would have just a few seconds to do it before the men inside began to react to the exterior explosion. All they knew about it was what they had been able to squeeze from Chuckie. Chuckie was a young, not too smart, member of the slavers' organization. They had spotted him with Feeney, the boss, when they made their rounds as far west as Chicago and as far south as Georgia to collect young women who had been 'harvested' by semi-independent groups scattered around the eastern half of the country. Since the girls had to be transported by truck, the trip back to New Jersey had to be able to be made within 24 hours or so. Otherwise you got into the need to feed and water the girls on the way. Too risky.

So they had picked up Chuckie about a week before. He had blubbered and cried when they threatened to shoot him. He gave up the whole operation. All that he knew, anyway. It was lucky for Jake and his crew that Chuckie had a family. Unbeknownst to his boss, he had fathered a little girl while in high school. Martinez had followed him there on one of his visits to the mother. Their lives were the price of Chuckie's cooperation. It was the only way to make him more afraid of them than of his boss. Chuckie described the interior of the building and how the team of slavers operated to load the large aluminum containers that the newly enslaved girls were shipped in. Once the last man arrived, the door to the basement would be opened and the girls would begin to be transferred to the loading platform. There was just big enough room to pull the industrial van in and close the garage door behind it.

The problem was that if the men inside were given more than a moment to react, they would retreat into the basement, shut the solid steel door and wait for reinforcements. They could easily dispose of anyone who tried to rush in even if the door to the basement was blown open. So Jake and his team had to get inside the loading area within seconds of blasting the outer door.

And they couldn't just run up across the street and load the explosives on the outer door. There was a security camera around each side of the building. If one of the slavers happened to be watching the video, he would warn the others and the operation would go snafu. That was where Mary Ellen and Leon came in. They had pulled Leon's big old Caddy opposite the door and had started to make out like nobody's business. The men who had walked down the street to enter the warehouse had barely taken notice of them. Mary Ellen was hot and they probably felt a touch of envy for the guy in the car as they passed by.

Now that all the men were in, Chuckie having called in 'sick', Mary Ellen and Leon broke their embrace. At the same time that the other men, Tucker, Curly, Martinez and Jake, made a dash for the door from across the street, Mary Ellen and Leon jumped from the Caddy and set the charges. They dove to the sides of the door and let them blow.

There was a large crashing sound, not unlike a car accident. Irving's silencers had worked like a charm. He had also designed spring loaded charges that could be shot against the garage door and triggered the second they hit. Four explosions followed the first by mere seconds. A hole the size of two men had been blown open and Jake and Martinez, leading the crew, jumped through it. It took Jake two seconds to run the length of the big brown van which had been backed into the loading area. He rounded the corner of the truck with his pistol raised.

The slavers were standing around, their mouths agape. Jake saw one make a movement to the cellar door and he cut him down with two shots from his nine millimeter. His body fell across the doorway blocking its closure. Martinez had run the length of the truck on the other side. He was an expert with the Uzi, and he gave out three short bursts and three other men were down. That left one more. He was probably in the cellar. Jake jumped through the door and rolled to the side. Three bullets whizzed by him. He came up in a crouch and sent a volley of shots across the room. While he was firing, Curly came through the door and jumped to the other side. Three more shots rang out, their noise deafening inside the small, block lined cellar. When Curley opened fire with his .306 shotgun, Jake jumped off of the landing and began to crawl along the wall. Martinez was in now too, and he kept the unknown gunman's head down with judicious short bursts.

They had been told of the girls who would be in the cages. Jake had carefully explained to his team, out of Irving's earshot, that they were expendable. But they were to try and be careful nonetheless.

There was a moment's silence in the small basement. Jake could hear the hooded and bound girls whining and crying behind their gags. There could be no mistaking the sounds of the shots, and even if their hearing was stifled by plugs in their ears, the fierce noise of the firing guns had to be discernable.

A voice yelled out from inside a small alcove at the end of the basement. "Don't shoot!" the man pleaded. "I give up!"

"Throw down your weapon," Jake called out to him. A few seconds later, the clatter of a handgun could be heard on the floor.

"Come out with your hands in the air over your head, palms facing me, fingers wide apart!" Jake instructed the man.

Feeney had been the only one to react at the sound of the first blast. He had had enough time to jump through the cellar door, but not enough time to shut it. He had retreated to the end of the cellar in a desperate hope that he could negotiate being taken alive.

When Feeney walked halfway down the length of the basement, his arms extended above him, his palms turned towards his captors, Jake rose from his supine position, his Glock was pointed directly at the man's heart.

Mary Ellen and Tucker were still in the loading area. They made sure that the downed men were permanently out of action. A large silver canister was open in the middle of the room. One of the bound and hooded girls was huddled on the floor, her body shaking. Three canisters had already been loaded. Mary Ellen controlled her impulse to comfort the crying girl at her feet. She was just merchandise, after all.

* * * * * * * * * * * * *

Four o'clock the following afternoon, local time, a small truck awaited entrance at the gate of a compound just three miles outside of Dlitski, the capital city of Kalikastan. Inside the truck was a large air cargo container. Inside the container were nine large aluminum canisters, used and useful in the transport of slave girls.

The compound belonged to a middle aged, fat man by the name of Khalid Rashini. Khalid might look comical, with his thinning black hair, his ample paunch. But he was a man of substance in Kalikastan. He was the main supplier of young, nubile, female slaves in the country. Kalikastan had devolved into a wide open, wide awake country following its separation from the Soviet Union. It is sandwiched between the new Russia and the Ukraine, and is a favorite source point of smuggled goods in and out of its two large neighbors. It's run mostly by loosely organized gangs, usually established along family or ethnic lines. They were almost impossible to penetrate and were utterly ruthless.

Aside from his nominal membership in one of the leading clans, Khalid was able to claim the bonds of commerce with most of the others. For his comely, young slave girls were in great demand. Kalikastan had become the favored vacation spot for most of the Eastern European underworld and some of the West. Dlitski itself was considered an 'open' city and as long as you minded your business, you could do anything you wanted there. The struggle for control of Kalikastan's criminal enterprises occurred mostly outside of the city.

So the Dlitski whorehouses were probably the best in the world. The well trained slave girls who staffed them would do anything, and you could do anything to them. And if one of them got damaged or hurt, she could always be replaced at Khalid's.

As the truck pulled into the huge courtyard of the compound, Khalid was busy in his suite of rooms, playing with two of his recently arrived guests. The suite was located on the second floor of one of the buildings that surrounded and blocked in the large cobblestone courtyard. He had a dingy, purely utilitarian office in the back. But the front consisted of a large salon, with comfortable cushions to lean against, a plush, thick oriental rug, a bar in the corner, several small tables and a number of tall floor lamps. Against the one wall were various wheeled devices for restraining young women. In the middle of the room a long chain descended from the ten foot high ceiling.

Khalid was sitting on the floor, leaning against one of the overstuffed pillows. He was wearing a pair of loose, white trousers and a striped sports shirt that was open to his navel. He had a large mat of thick black hair on his chest and he sported a large, thick, black moustache on his upper lip.

Before him were kneeling two bound and gagged, young slave girls. This was an Italian lot, just in from Naples. The girls both had jet black hair and dark olive skinned bodies. The one on the right, Luciana, had hair that was short but thick, styled into large ringlets all over her head. She had small, coffee cup sized breasts that stood firm and pert on her thin frame. The other girl, Francesca, was a little heavier built, not plump, just more filled out. She had graceful, wide hips and large, bulbous breasts. Her nipples were long and thick and they were hard from fear as she faced this unknown man. Her hair was long and straight and it reached down to the middle of her back. She had a small tattoo on the back of her left shoulder, a tiny bluebird.

The women had their arms tied behind their backs with leather thongs and had leather masks over their lower faces with long, thick gags in their mouths. They had been here for a little over a day. Yesterday, they had witnessed Khalid welcoming their shipment of pretty young girls with a traditional whipping of one of the luckless females, picked, more or less, at random. They had been raped by the guards repeatedly. They now had no illusions as to why they had been brought to Khalid's den of iniquity.

"Well, my pretties," Khalid said in English. He had one of his lieutenants check with the new girls as to who spoke English and these two foolishly raised their hands, probably thinking that that earned them some kind of favored treatment. What it bought them was an afternoon of torment from their new, if temporary, owner.

"We're going to play a little game," Khalid continued. "One of you is going to get whipped this afternoon." The girl's faces cringed at the news. They waited to hear more.

"You," Khalid said, pointing at Francesca, "you will sit on my lap. Come here now," he ordered.

The heavy breasted, naked girl hesitated for just one instant and then walked on her knees to where Khalid sat. He bid her to turn around and then pulled her to sit on his folded legs. Khalid's face broke into a greasy grin. He had a large gold tooth and it sparkled in the light. He placed his hands on Francesca's breasts and pinched her turgid nipples. "Beautiful, my little whore. You have beautiful tits."

The luscious girl squirmed on Khalid's lap. Her hands, bound behind her, were pressed into his stomach. He pulled her back against his chest and then spread her legs wide with his hands. Francesca, a music student, had been on her way to a concert. She had met a man the day before near the conservatory. He was handsome and sophisticated.

He made her laugh. They made a date. When he pulled up in his luxurious, black sedan, she smiled at him and got in the passenger door. As she looked over at him to say 'hello', a hand holding a damp, odiferous cloth clamped over her nose and mouth. She inhaled in surprise and fright. That was the last thing she remembered before she found herself naked and bound in a small cage. She never saw the man again.

The girl's thighs were thick and firm, her stomach taut. She had a large, hairy black bush surrounding her pussy that spread over onto her thighs and reached high on her tummy. She was embarrassed that it had been so prominently displayed over the last week or so, the time during which she spent caged in a Neapolitan cellar, awaiting shipment. None of the other girls she had seen were so endowed, a few had even shaved there. She had always enjoyed the animalistic feeling her thick thatch brought her, so she had left it alone. She had never thought that she would have to exhibit it so openly to strangers.

Once Francesca had been comfortably settled on his lap, Khalid turned to the other girl. "Now the rules of the game are that you," he said, pointing to Luciana, "are going to suck on this one's hairy cunt. You will have fifteen minutes to make her come three times." Luciana blanched at this news. She was only nineteen and had lived in a small village northeast of Naples all her life. She had been schooled under the auspices of the Sisters of the Holy Veil. Cunnilingus was not on the curriculum. She had been in the city to visit an Aunt and had gotten on the wrong bus. She ended up down by the docks. The bus was going out of service and so she was left off there all alone. She wasn't alone for very long.

In any case, she had never done such a thing in her life. She had made love with one boy and he had never even tried to do it to her. It was disgusting, she thought. She looked up at the depraved man in disbelief, her eyes wide over her masked face. Khalid sensed her hesitation.

"Never sucked a pussy before, my dear?" The girl shook her head 'no', miserably. "Well then, its time you learned. Unless, that is, you wish to give up the game and take a turn on the whipping chain, eh?"

The girl looked at the chain that dangled down from the ceiling next to her. She had seen Khalid whipping that pretty little blond girl yesterday. She definitely did not want to get whipped. Her bound hands were sweating behind her back. A tear floated down her cheek.

"Now, as for you," Khalid said to the young girl on his lap, "if she should win, then you will lose. I'll flog those pretty plump breasts of yours until you scream. Okay?"

Francesca didn't think it was okay, but she didn't want to give this strange man any further justification to abuse her. Khalid's hands were wandering over her heavy globes and her widespread thighs. His head leaned over the girl's shoulder. "And since your friend here is handicapped by not having any experience, I'm going to get you going, kind of give her a running start." His fat hand lodged between Francesca's thighs. He pushed aside the morass of black hair and put his fingers between her labial lips. He stroked them softly as he manipulated one of her breasts with his other hand.

The long haired Italian girl tried to fight off the effects of Khalid's ministrations to her body. She closed her eyes and thought of how she hated him and all the men who had abused her since she had been kidnapped. She tried to build the hatred so high so as to push out any other thoughts. And it worked for a while. But, finally, her sex began to moisten and fill with blood. Khalid's fingers were able to slide easily into the crevasse between her thighs. She gave an involuntary moan.

"Okay," Khalid announced. "She's ready!" He motioned the other girl to come closer. "Hurry," he told her, "or she'll go off the boil."

Luciana bent her head as Khalid removed her gag. When she looked up, her eyes were filled with moisture, her face forlorn. She was kneeling between her target's thighs. Khalid had a 15 minute timer on the floor next to him. He had played this game before. He set the alarm. "Now, go!" he yelled.

The curly haired girl looked startled for a moment, unsure of what to do. The chain dangling from the ceiling was right next to her. She glanced at it ruefully, and then bent down quickly to seize Francesca's cunt with her mouth.

Khalid had pushed Francesca's torso down so that her back was in an arch. This presented her loins for her competitor's hot tongue. Luciana barely knew where to start, but she remembered what she liked to feel the few times that she had sinfully stroked herself down there and she acted accordingly. She was almost overpowered by the heavy musk scent emitted by Francesca's moist hole. She began to tickle the little bud at the top of the girl's sex with her tongue. Francesca stiffened as she felt the unwelcome increase in her arousal. She sighed as Luciana dragged her broad tongue the length of her slit. She moaned when, in a moment of inspiration, Luciana took her little bud in her mouth and sucked on it gently.

Khalid noted the excitement of the girl on his lap. He had continued to play with her tits, pinching the nipples, caressing them. "Getting horny, slut?" he asked her.

Francesca's gag was still in place and so she could not respond, but her body told the tale. Her breasts had become hard and her skin taut. A great splotch of red had broken out on her chest. Her breath was coming uneven and in deep, heavy pants.

Luciana did not know how much time had gone by, but she was beginning to lose faith that she could do it. Her face was buried in the tangled jungle of Francesca's pubic hair. Desperately she massaged Francesca's slit with her tongue. She began to literally lap at the girl's clitoris, brushing it each time with her plump lips. At this she felt the young girl stiffen. She increased her pace. She heard Khalid call out, "Nine minutes, little Lucy, six more to go."

Suddenly, Francesca was forced to give into the pleasure that had been gnawing at her will to resist. Her body took over as her juicy crevasse ejaculated a stream of her viscous juices across Luciana's face. "Oh!" she cried as she felt her pussy contract. "Oh! Oh! Oh!" she called out through her gag, a wave of pleasure washing over her.

Khalid had felt the girl's body stiffen and then begin to writhe and jerk. "One!" he declared laughing. He grabbed Francesca's breasts and stroked them, tickling her nipples and massaging the ample orbs. "Two to go!"

Luciana continued her oral efforts at Francesca's cunt. She started by pushing her tongue deep into Francesca's slit and drawing her tongue up and over the tender spot on top. She continued with long, continuous strokes. Francesca had never really cooled off, and the lavish attention her pussy was receiving reignited her lust. She tried to fight it off, closing her eyes, cursing and swearing under her breath. Several more minutes went by as she tottered on the edge of passion. Luciana took her tiny bud of pleasure between her teeth and nipped at it, pulling it to its length, tonguing its tender tip. This time, Francesca exploded in orgasm. Her hips began to rock and her body jerked. Her eyes rolled back. "Ahhhhhhhhhhhhh!" she yelled through her mask in the heat of her passion. "Ahhhhhhhhhhhh! Ahhhhhhhhhhhhh!" she moaned, in Italian, of course.

There were a little over four minutes to go. Luciana hardened her tongue into a firm weapon and began to stroke Francesca's clit repeatedly in a downward direction. She let it drag over the little, hard nubbin as would a stiff manhood. Again and again she raised and lowered her head. Khalid, sensing that Francesca might try to close her legs, extended his and encircled her ankles with his.

Realizing that he last ditch defense was taken from her, Francesca began to moan and whine behind her gag. Her legs were jerking and her thighs quivering.

Khalid looked down at the sweet Luciana. Her bound hands, behind her, resting on the small of her back just before the gracious curves of her ass, were opening and closing frantically as she made a panicked, strenuous effort to bring Francesca off one more time. Almost mechanically, like a piston, her head bobbed up and down, pushing her firm tongue against Francesca's pleasure bud, rasping it down its length.

"Twenty Seconds!" Khalid called out. He was rubbing his open palms on Francesca's nipples which were as hard as pencil points. "Fifteen!" he yelled.

Francesca was starting to take in deep breaths. She desperately tried to push her legs closed, frustrated by Khalid's. She started to moan, her voice muffled by her gag. "Mmmmpf! Mmmmmmpf! Mmmmmmpf! Mmmmmmmmmpf!" she went, each expression of lust louder than the last.

"Ten seconds!" Khalid announced. Suddenly Francesca gave an anguished cry. Her body convulsed and her hips rocked up against the tongue that was tormenting her. "Ohhhhhhhhhhhhhh!" she moaned deeply in her throat. "Ohhhhhhhhhhhhhhhh!"

Just as Francesca gave her second long, miserable moan, the timer went off, emitting a loud ring. Khalid picked it up and put it next to Francesca's ear as the girl's body shuddered and quaked. "Oh, you almost made it," he told her tauntingly. "But I was rooting for Luciana here. I just couldn't resist the thought of putting my whip to your tender breasts."

Francesca began to cry even as her third orgasm continued to rock her body. Luciana raised her head from between the other girl's thighs. Her face was smeared with Francesca's juices. She began to cry as well, but tears of relief. She would not be whipped. At least not today. At least not right now.

Khalid seemed to shift gears. He pushed Francesca's head down sharply until she was bent over. Holding her neck still with one hand, he loosened the straps around her wrists with the other. The girl quickly pulled her hands loose and tried to struggle away. But Khalid grabbed her arms with his powerful hands and held them out in front of the girl, locking her torso still with his huge, thick legs.

"Come here!" he ordered Luciana. She hesitated briefly, but fear took the better of her and she complied. "Turn your back to me!" the cruel slaver roared. When she had done so, he captured Francesca's wrists with one vice-like hand and loosened Luciana's bonds with the other.

"Get the chain," he yelled at her. Luciana scurried to comply. It was dangling only a few feet away. There were two leather bracelets on the end of it. Khalid held

Francesca's wrists out to the other girl. "Put them on her!" he boomed.

Luciana was hesitant to become complicit in the other girl's torture, but she still complied dutifully. She was crying and sobbing, frightened by the large man's wrath. She knew that in a trice she could be the one getting the beating, contest or no contest. She had dirtied and humiliated herself to avoid that. She would do whatever the fat man said or her degradation would have been in vain.

Once the bracelets were in place on the struggling girl's wrists, Khalid pushed her off of his lap. He quickly stood and pulled on the other end of the chain. Holding it firmly, he backed up to the wall and let the chain raise Francesca first to her knees and then to her feet. When her toes barely touched the ground, he ran a link of the chain through a hook on the wall.

Francesca squirmed and twisted in almost mindless fear. She was going to be whipped! Her whole insides revolted at the thought of such cruel, deliberate abuse. "What have I done to deserve this?" she thought miserably. "Why is this happening?"

The answer to her questions were nothing, she had done nothing except to be an unprotected, pretty, young woman all alone. And why? Because it gave her owner pleasure.

Khalid took a tasseled whip from the wall. It would sting like the blazes, but would leave only deeply reddened skin. These girls were for the market in a few days and he didn't want them all marked up. Francesca's tits would be raw and sore for a day or so, but the redness would dissipate.

Luciana was kneeling on the floor unsure of what to do. She had received no orders and she knew not to do anything without permission.

"Come over here." Khalid answered callously. Luciana knelt at his feet. "I'm going to give you a chance to redeem yourself," Khalid told her. He had undone his fly and his not quite yet hardened cock slipped out. "I'm going to give this whore five strokes across the tits. Then you will give me five strokes with your mouth. When you get me off, I'll stop beating her. Got that?"

Luciana trembled at the thought of the man's hard penis in her mouth. But she looked at the miserable Francesca. She hardly knew the girl, had never spoken to her. She had only seen her as a gagged and caged prisoner like herself while they were held in some dingy basement awaiting transport, and yesterday in the courtyard as they were forced to service the men of the establishment with their mouths, on their knees. The nineteen year old Catholic convent girl was wracked with guilt. Her own despicable act of oral stimulation of her loins had sealed Francesca's fate. She had to do anything she could to relieve it.

The abject girl nodded mournfully at the formidable man. She looked at his long, thick cock and she wondered if she could do it. Could she really put that thing in her mouth?

The slaver reared back his right arm and proceeded to lay a fierce blow of the whip across Francesca's breasts. The skin was immediately transformed to a bright pink where the lashes had struck. Francesca's body stiffened and she screamed behind her gag. Her long, graceful legs swung freely as her body convulsed from the blow.

Khalid delivered four more powerful blows of the whip to Francesca's meaty breasts. She screamed and yelled, her muffled voice filling the room. When the fifth blow had been administered, Khalid turned to the kneeling, trembling girl at his feet. He grabbed her by the back of the head and told her, "Open your mouth, cunt." Luciana complied and then seized Khalid's now steel hard cock with her lips. She was crying as his pole slid into her mouth, depressing her tongue. She barely knew how to do this and she only had five strokes to bring this beast to orgasm, she thought desperately.

In actuality, it was not as bad as it sounded. Khalid relished beating a pretty young woman. At each stroke, his cock got harder and harder. He could come just watching a screaming female suffer. It was almost as if shoving his hot meat in Luciana's mouth would cool him off. And it had the salutary effect of spreading Francesca's torture out over a longer time.

As he drew his cock across Luciana's lips, he moaned softly, giving her hope. She sucked hard on the meaty pole as it withdrew and greeted it with her tongue when it returned. When Khalid had finished his fifth stroke in her eager mouth, she was bitterly disappointed.

The cruel slave trader laid five more blows over Francesca's almost beet red breasts. She howled like a wounded animal at each stroke. Five more times he plundered Luciana's pursed lips with his meat.

Altogether, Khalid let the little game play out for five full rounds. After he had laid leather to Francesca's tormented tits for the twenty fifth time, he turned and grabbed Luciana by her short, curly black hair. Gripping it firmly, he pushed her mouth down hard on his cock. The girl squealed as it pressed past the entrance to her throat.

Khalid pulled out, only to push in again, rubbing Luciana's nose against his pubic bone. Luciana cried and sobbed as she was being abused. On the fifth stroke, Khalid, a true master of his cock, pushed down deep into Luciana's esophagus. He held her there, impaled on his joint. She started to struggle for air. Suddenly, his cock exploded. Quick, hard tremors flew through his body. He became barely conscious of the desperate girl whose airway he blocked. Jet after jet of his salty, white spewm he sent down her throat. The girl was struggling for air, pounding her fists on his knees and thighs, frantic that she would die with this man's cock deep inside her mouth. But Khalid did not unnecessarily damage stock in trade. He pulled out just before Luciana fainted. As it was, her eyes were beginning to flutter and her jaw to slacken. She breathed in a deep, desperately needed chestfull of air.

Just then there was a frantic knock on Khalid's door.

"Pasha Rashini! You must come! Please, please!"

It was Achmed, his sister's cousin. "He's lucky he didn't come a minute earlier," Khalid thought. Why he had to employ these mealy mouthed relatives was beyond him. What could be so serious?

Khalid took a moment to hogtie Luciana and to restore her gag. "I'll be back to fuck you in a while," he told her. "And then the whip for you!"

Luciana gave out a mournful moan.

Khalid followed the man across the courtyard to the building where the slaves were released from their canisters. They were usually allowed to sit closed for a while so that the young female prisoners inside could begin to emerge from their drugged fogs. They had apparently just been opened. "What can be wrong?" Khalid asked himself, worried now. "Are they all dead?"

As he entered the room, he saw the canisters lying next to each other, lined up down the hallway. He looked at the first four. They were filled with sandbags, simulating the weight of a woman's body. But was the fifth through ninth that really caught his eye. In each one of the last five canisters lay a male body. That they had died of gunshot wounds was clear. Each one lay in a pool of his own dried blood. He recognized the last one, Feeney. He had a little hole in the middle of his forehead.

Khalid went into an unmitigated rage. He stomped and cursed, his face turning beet red. He grabbed a whip from the wall and started belaying the messenger. Achmed trembled as he absorbed the blows. Finally, Khalid's anger had run its course. He looked up to see his major domo and right hand man, Sergi, looking back at him. He was tall and muscular. He had his hands folded across his broad chest. He had eyes that could bore a hole in steel. Suddenly, Khalid burst into laughter. His belly shook and his eyes began to tear. It was if he'd gone mad. After a minute, he was able to get a hold on himself. Smiling, his mirth just below the surface, he said, "Sergi, it looks like we have a new partner. Get on a plane to New York right away."

CHAPTER THREE

Maddy lay awake lying on her thin, cotton pallet for a long time that night after her master's assault on her rear passage. Her collar and ankles were anchored to the floor and thick straps had been fixed around her thighs and lower legs. She could still feel her anal ring extended, slowly contracting to its normal size. She was dismally unhappy that her trainer had made her impale herself on his cock and that he had been able to force her to climax by fucking her there. She knew that he would do it again and again, until her ass became another source of sexual pleasure for her. Perhaps even a preferred one.

The unhappy ponygirl knew that these men had taken control of her body from her. But now she realized that they had possession of her mind as well. They were making her into something else, something strange, half woman, half beast. She was frightened that she would lose all that she ever had, that this reality would replace the old one, and that soon her memories of her past life would seem as strange to her as her reality did now.

Already she was having trouble picturing the people in her former life. Her father, her boyfriend, her girlfriends. Their faces seemed like the stars that you can see at night only if you look away at them. There, but not there. Not subject to scrutiny.

And there was the sex. Could she really call it rape when each time a man plunged a hard cock into her she creamed? Was her body even real? She could not see it, she could hardly move it. She shook her shoulders slightly just to feel the sway of her breasts. But were they hers if she could never touch them? They existed for the enjoyment of others, and the pleasure that she received when hot lips pulled at her nipples, or heavy hands caressed her buoyant orbs, was only to a purpose not her own. She knew that men enjoyed handling breasts, were somehow mesmerized by their softness, their malleability. And so she brought these men pleasure when they placed their mouths and hands on her globes. But she also knew that the men were using her own body to reshape her mind. That the pleasure she received from the gentle tug of lips on her teats, the hands on her sex, the lips on her tender pleasure bud, was designed to drive out all else. All thoughts, all wants, all needs. All that was to be left was the physical experience of the moment. Like a beast, she would have no thought for the future or the past. She would only be. And what she would be was what they wanted her to be.

To her utter shame, her body still yearned to be possessed. It was as if once alone, she ceased to exist. She could not move on her own, she could not eat or drink on her own. She could not even perform her most intimate bodily functions alone. So without the men, the others, she was nothing, a shell, a toy waiting for a hand to set it in motion.

She pledged to herself not to give in, not to surrender. She would hold on to a kernel of hate. Since her past was gone and, seemingly, never to be recovered, she could not hold on to love. The persons who had been loved and who had loved her were gone forever. But there was hate. She would hate them all forever, all of her tormentors. She would never give in to them, never allow her kernel of self to wither away.

Maddy didn't know it, but she was experiencing the same emotions that had been felt by each of the young women who had been turned into ponies. The battle could only end one way.

The unhappy pony finally fell asleep, and when she awoke the barn was already full of activity. A man came into her stall and removed the flaps covering her eyes. It was one of the stable boys. Since it was no longer raining, after disposing of her bodily wastes, she would be taken out for her morning run. She determined that she would not be last today.

The bevy of ponies was led up to the track by the trainers and their helpers. Maddy joined the others as they stretched their legs in anticipation. The small gathering of naked, blue helmeted, faceless females looked like a flock of pigeons as they jerked their heads this way and that in order to see out of their tiny eye holes. Although the track was generally dry, there were large puddles that had not yet evaporated or drained away. By mid afternoon they would be gone. Maddy made note of the puddles, resolving not to step in them.

All of a sudden they were off. Maddy tried to keep up with the pack, leaning her shoulders forward, pumping her thighs as high and as fast as they would go. It was difficult to learn to run fast with your hands bound behind you, but Maddy had had a lot of practice over the last ten days. After she had been out running on the track a couple of times, she had learned to keep her head down and her shoulders still. In doing this, she realized why the collars were tilted up in the front. When the chin rested on the raised edge of the front the collar, and she leaned forwards to pick up speed, her face was in precisely the right place, her eyes poised to view her narrow goal: to be first.

As they rounded the far turn, Maddy started falling behind. Just ahead of her was one of the huge carriage ponies, used for hauling the larger vehicles in a team, or a small trap all by themselves. Her long, brown pony tail flitted back and forth as she ran. Maddy could see the strong muscles working in her haunches as she dug her toes into the track to propel her bulk forward. Suddenly, the pony ahead of her seemed to slip sideways. She had placed her boot on the edge of a puddle and it had slid out from under her on the mud. The pony crashed to the ground not three yards ahead of Maddy. She did not have time to avoid her and she tied to jump over. Her boot caught the other pony's arm and she fell, face forwards, her body fully extended. She slid right through a large puddle. But rather than stopping to assess the damage, she quickly rolled over and pushed herself back onto her feet by sheer will. She was covered from head to foot in dripping brown water and oozing mud. She hit her feet running.

The trainers who had been watching gave out a great cheer. Others drifted over to the track to see what the commotion was. Maddy had a forty yard lead on the pony that had tripped her. She dug into the track with her toes as hard as she could. Her chest felt near to bursting as she drove herself forward. She could only see directly ahead of her through the small holes in her hood and she kept the center of the track in sharp focus.

As she entered the home stretch, the other pony was right behind her. Ten or twenty of the staff were gathered at the finish line. They were hooting and hollering, urging her on. There were a hundred meters left, then fifty, then thirty. The big brown haired pony was just at her shoulder.

Maddy seized all of the energy left in her body and expended it in one last desperate burst of speed. She crossed the finish line half a step in front of the other pony.

There was a tumult of celebration. She had given the men great sport. Men slapped her on her mud covered shoulders and rubbed the top of her head. She was close to collapsing from her efforts and she felt herself held up by a strong pair of hands. She looked up. At first she could see only part of a face through the tiny holes, but then, by shuddering her head around like a stop action film, she saw that it was her trainer and he was grinning widely.

As the men broke away from her, laughing and recounting for themselves Maddy's heroic race, she saw the other pony being led over to the rail where, for many days running, she had leaned over and taken the penalty for being last. Maddy felt a clip being attached to her collar and she was pulled away from the scene of her triumph, as small as it was. But it was a start.

To Drabik, it was a sign of heart. All great athletes, even horses and ponygirls, needed heart. It was something that drove you to exceed the possible. And he saw that, as he had suspected, Maddy had it.

He led the still recovering pony down the pathway to the training area. Drabik stopped and turned around. He gave Maddy the hand signal for kneeling, the snap of the fingers down at the level of his waist. Maddy responded as if by instinct. Drabik looked at her. She was a glorious mess. And now for her reward.

Drabik unbuttoned his fly and removed his cock from his pants. Maddy watched in anticipation. He leaned over and unfastened her gag from behind her head. He removed her gag and tossed it to the ground. He gave the curt, verbal command that signified for Maddy to open her lips and receive him.

For the past seven days but one, the day it rained, every morning, after her dismal performance on the track, he had led Maddy to this very same spot. Each of those mornings he had fastened her collar to a post and given her ten sharp blows from a whip. But today there was no whip. Today was special. Maddy would get to please her master.

And that was exactly what Maddy was feeling when the head of his cock passed over her lips. In her exhilaration, she wanted nothing more than to please this man who was forming her, perfecting her. She knew that the strength that she had found to burst forward at the last second had been built under his supervision in her daily circuits around the training wheel.

Maddy closed her eyes as she inhaled Drabik's manhood. She felt a thrill in her loins as she twirled her tongue around it. Her featureless, blue clad head churned slowly back and forth, her useless hands, clenched tightly in their confinements behind her. Usually, Drabik placed his hands on her head, guiding her movements up and down. But today his hands were on his hips. The only contact between them was between lips and prick. It was Maddy's day, she could suck him for as long as and in any way she pleased.

Maddy's mind clouded over with a feeling of fulfillment as she worked her lips and tongue up and down the length of Drabik's shaft. His cock was hot and delicious. She pressed her face forward as far as it would go, taking his length into her throat, and then, slowly, almost lovingly pulled back, exciting every square inch of his skin. She placed her lips on the fat, round head and sucked on it, running her tongue over the little crevice on the underside.

Drabik moaned with pleasure. He realized that this was a turning point in Maddy's conversion to a servile beast. From here on in it was just a matter of time. He looked at the mud covered pony. She would yearn to please him and she would race, race like her life depended on it, race for him, her master.

The young pony continued to massage her lips over her master's manhood. She had a vision of herself kneeling there, supine and abject, faceless, anonymous, naked to the world, but at total harmony with herself. She could actually picture her blue lined jaw working as she took in her master's swollen prick.

Suddenly, she began to yearn for the taste of his sperm. It was hers to draw out, to savor, to enjoy. She pressed her lips down hard on Drabik's cock, moaning her pleasure. She pumped her head back and forth, gaining momentum as she went. Drabik felt his seed being drawn from his sac, felt the impending crescendo. When he came, he gave a shout. He placed his hands on Maddy's shoulders and pumped back madly at her mouth. As for Maddy, when she heard her master groan and felt his cock begin to throb, her own pussy began to pulse and contract with pleasure.

After drawing out every drop of her master's seed, Maddy finally surrendered his softening tool back to him.

Before bringing Maddy out to the training track, after washing, feeding and grooming her, Drabik produced a thin leather belt. He attached it around her waist, locking it in place. Maddy had never seen any of the other ponies wearing one and so she wondered what it was for. Drabik then pulled from his pocket a small, white, narrow, triangular cup. It had thin chains affixed to each of its corners and its surface was made of a thin screen. He clipped one of the chains to the center of the belt in front.

He then lowered the cup and placed it over Maddy's hairless mound. He placed the two golden disks that hung there inside of it. The other two chains he drew up over her rear flanks. He fastened them tightly in place so that the cup pressed up hard against Maddy's groin. When he was satisfied that her cunt was completely covered and that nothing could be slipped between the cup and her skin, he placed little padlocks on the chains. He then stood up and placed the same little locks on her bridle.

He pulled Maddy over to the training wheel and hooked her up for the start of her exercise. Maddy contemplated the purpose of the locks holding the cup taut against her mons and on her bridle, she came to the realization of what he had done. Last night he had used her rear opening to drive her to physical pleasure. From now until he released her chains and locks, anyone who wanted to use her would need to plow that path. Her mouth and her sex would be locked away, available only at her master's whim.

Drabik worked her hard that day. Three times during the morning and twice in the afternoon, other trainers stopped by to make use of her. Drabik would release her from the training wheel and lead her over to the grass. A snap of his fingers and she lowered herself to her knees. Another snap and she placed her forehead on the ground, spreading her legs.

When the first man mounted her that morning, she felt the same revulsion and dismay at this perverse use of her body as she always had. Her tiny ring stretched painfully as he entered her. He sawed away at her ass, seeking only his own pleasure. When he was done, his seed splashed deep in her bowels, Drabik snapped his fingers again, this time up by his shoulders. She rose to her knees and then, on the second snap, to her feet.

At each use, her anal ring seemed to become more and more sensitized. By the end of the day, as she knelt, her backside proffered to the anonymous male, she moaned when the hot prick pierced her. Her fires started to burn as the thick rod dragged across the tight circle of tactile flesh. When he came, her lusts were still rising. Her pussy tingled with yearning, her blood was hot.

The next day, she lost the race again, and the day after that, too. On the third day, she had fallen three lengths behind the hindmost pony. After she had taken her five at the rail, Drabik, instead of taking her to the training area, brought her back to the barn. He left her standing there, her nose ring tied to a post until all of the ponies and trainers had left. He untied the ring and dragged her over to the center of the barn. He stepped to the wall that divided the central area from the stalls and released a chain from a hook. One end of the chain came tumbling down from the ceiling and landed at Maddy's feet.

Maddy's heart froze over with fear. She had been whipped at this chain the day of her arrival. She had writhed in agonized pain as he tormented her cruelly, her screams of pain muffled by her gag. She had been whipped since, daily, really. But never again like that. She looked at her master and saw the cold determination in his eyes. She started to tremble. As he released her arms from behind her back, she lost control of her bladder.

Drabik, ignoring the pony's release of her water, attached the chain to the bracelets on her wrists. It was ironic that her arms were of no use to her as a ponygirl with the sole exception of preparing her for a tortuous whipping. Maddy felt her hands pulled over her head until she was lifted to her toes. She immediately felt the strain on her muscle depleted arms. She was crying.

Drabik fastened a belt around Maddy's ankles and then tied it to a ring in the floor. She would be unable to move her feet or sway to avoid the impact of the whip. He selected a six foot long lash. It had been soaked in vinegar and it had grown hard and twisted. He reared his arm back and slashed the whip against Maddy's skin.

The first blow was received across her upper thighs. It was like someone had drawn a ragged knife across them. Maddy's screamed in pain. Her gagged mouth worked in a futile attempt to form words, to beg for mercy. When the second lash was laid across her breasts, Maddy howled in pain. As he had on the first day, Drabik slowly circled the distended pony. He struck out randomly, without warning. Maddy tried to keep her eyes glued to him as he strolled about her and every 20 seconds or so unleashed a world of pain on her body. He was relentless in his efficiency, marking every part of her with long, angry, red welts. Her breasts were criss-crossed with red lines. Three times he reversed direction so that he could reach parts of her body inaccessible from the other.

When he stopped, Maddy was sobbing inconsolably. It was ten times worse than her first whipping. She had thought that her body was about to burst into flame. Maddy hardly knew that her torment was over when Drabik released her wrists from the chain. He refastened them to their normal position behind her back and then pushed her to her knees. He unlocked her gag from behind her head and pulled it from her mouth. He withdrew his long, thick cock from his pants and uttered the command. Maddy at first didn't hear it. He slapped her across her sore, tortured breasts and repeated it. Obediently she spread her lips apart and took him in.

All she could think of as he plundered her mouth was, 'This is the cock of the man who just whipped me!" Her body still burned from her lashing. Drabik guided her hooded head's movements by holding her ponytail in his hand. He pushed her face against his loins, entering her throat. Twice, when her service seemed to lag, he withdrew his prick and slapped her defenseless tits again viciously.

Maddy could not stop crying as Drabik's meaty cock filled her mouth. Only a few days ago she had performed this act with joy. Now she knelt in utter debasement, an anonymous face docilely receiving his thrusts, her lips obediently pursed around his shaft. Finally, he spilled himself into her mouth. He groaned as her warm wetness encircled him.

When he was done, Drabik restored Maddy's thick, leather gag. He snapped his fingers at the height of his shoulders and Maddy rose to her feet obediently. He led her from the barn with a leash over to the training wheel. He removed her gag and installed her bit and bridle. He connected it to the wheel and turned on the motor. Maddy felt her face pulled forward and she began to run.

That was the last time that Maddy finished last in the race. During the night, she concentrated her whole mind on running, running, running. Her body was atingle as she was led to the track the next morning, thatched with angry red lines, evidence of the prior day's abuse. When the whistle blew she started to run and put everything behind her.

CHAPTER FOUR

Jake's mind was on money as he sat in the reclining chair in the manager's office of the Elizabeth Uniform Company. The office had an old style, wooden, swiveled office chair, a steel desk covered with bills of lading and invoices and a large map of the eastern half United States on the wall. Jake had never thought that someday he would be operating a real business. But, once they had squeezed out of Feeney everything he knew, and then put a hole in him, someone had to take the reins of the front for the slave girl operation. In the morning he merely called a meeting of the drivers and other managers and told them that he had bought the business and for everybody to continue to do as they were doing. He thought that that took care of everything.

That afternoon, Felix Montoya, the assistant operations manager, came to him. He was about 55 years old. He had a receding line of short, black curly hair. He looked like a guy who had worked all his life, dotting every 'i', crossing every 't'. He wore wire rimmed glasses over his brown face. He was thin, about 5'9". He showed Jake some papers. "If we don't so something about this, you'll be bankrupt in a month."

Jake looked up at him from his squeaky reclining chair with perplexity. Did Feeney really run this place, he wondered. "Why?" was all he said.

"Because you're paying out more than you bring in. That's why," Felix answered.

"And how does that happen?" Jake asked, amazed that anyone would talk to him about something like this.

"You're not charging enough for uniforms, for one," Felix responded. "And there's too many lost goods, you know, unreturned."

"What do you mean unreturned? Jake asked. "Why would we want people to return the uniforms? Is there something wrong with them?"

Felix looked at Jake like he had two heads. "Do you know that you bought a uniform rental company?" He put the emphasis on 'rental'.

"Yeah, sure," Jake answered. No, he didn't know that.

"Well, do you understand that when you rent things to people they're supposed to give them back?" Felix asked, his eyes searching Jake's for any sign of intelligence.

"Of course," Jake replied, trying to recover some of his authority.

"Well, too many people haven't been giving them back. The company's losing money on each rental. We're supposed to charge people for not giving the clothes back."

"Well, that sounds okay to me?" Jake said trying to sound executive-like.

"But Mr. Wilson, or whatever you name is......" Felix started, his voice reaching a high level of exasperation.

Jake waived his hand for him to stop. "Montoya, that's your name, right."

Felix looked at Jake. He paused. He looked Jake in the eye. "Listen, mister, if you're going to fire me then do it, because I can't...."

Jake waived his hand again. "How much do you make, Mr. Montoya?"

"Well," Felix thought to himself, "if he's going to pull this 'I make more than you so I'm smarter' routine, I might as well quit right now".

"$55,000," he told Jake.

"Well," Jake said, "now you're making $95,000. Do what you need to do. I don't want to hear about anything. I've taken over Mr. Feeney's supplemental operations. I have very powerful friends. You stay on your side of the garage door and I'll stay on mine. Okay?"

Felix looked at him, dumbfounded. "Wha...," he started to say.

"If the business needs any cash, call me at this number." Jake handed him a business card with his answering service number on it.

"Well, okay," Felix mumbled. Jake got out of the chair and started to walk out. "B,but what about the bank accounts, I can't sign the checks," Felix pointed out, following behind Jake to the door.

Jake turned around. "There'll be new signature cards here tomorrow. Do what needs to be done." Jake paused. He looked Felix in the eye. "And don't fuck with us, okay? And if any of my people need a truck, you give it to them. Got it?"

"Okay, Mr......"

"Just Jake." He turned to leave again, but remembered something important.

"In the next couple of days a guy with a Russian accent is going to come and see me about some overseas shipments. Call me right away when he arrives."

Jake returned to the lower regions of the building. He would make a note to have Burnham send this guy some cash so the business could stay afloat. Mary Ellen was down there with Chuckie. All the other guys were running security up and down the block in case anybody who missed Feeney came calling. You never could tell. Irving he had sent home. Irving didn't have the moxie for what had to be done next.

Chuckie looked a little downtrodden. He had never worked for a lady before and it took some getting used to. Especially when she called you a balless fuck, or pencil dick. He was ashamed of how he cried and begged to live when Jake's gang had picked him up. And he was surrounded by beautiful, naked women and he couldn't fuck any of them.

"Hey, gutless," Jake said as he came in.

Chuckie's shoulders slumped. "Oh, that's not nice, Mr. Wilson. I never did any…."

"Stuff it Chuckie," Jake said. "I'm here to talk to your boss. So go outside and play." He worried a little about Chuckie. He was a weak link. Anybody could find out what they had, about his kid and all. But for the time being, they needed him.

Jake waited for Chuckie to leave before talking to Mary Ellen. He looked over her sylvan charms. "Boy," he thought. "She sure looks hot."

"I wouldn't have believed if I hadn't seen it with my own eyes," Mary Ellen said. She was referring to the line of cages against the wall, each of which contained a shapely young female, bound and hooded.

"Me neither," Jake said. "Are you up for this?" he asked the tall, desirable, yellow haired woman.

She shrugged her shoulders. "I've done worse," she replied.

"I don't know how long that we'll have to keep the operation going, but it could be months. We're talking probably dozens of girls. And they had more than one customer. Do you think you can handle handing over these innocent young things to cruel and barbarous masters?"

"Cruel and barbarous masters? You been reading something?"

"No, but it's not far from the truth."

"So what," Mary Ellen replied. "If we didn't take them somebody else would. And if it wasn't these girls, it would be some other girls. We'll keep 'em comfy, we won't beat them and we won't rape them. We'll just sell them."

Jake paused to take in the ruthlessness of one of the most ruthless people he knew. "I expect to hear from the overseas buyers within 24 hours. Can you ship right after that?"

"Yeah, I have a few of my girlfriends coming down. We can handle it. What I can't handle is Chuckie." Mary Ellen was strictly gay.

"We need him for the moment," Jake told her. "He'll introduce you to the sellers, make them more comfortable dealing with you. When you think you've got all from him you need, you can do what you want."

"That suits me," Mary Ellen said. "Which brings up one more thing."

"What's that."

"There's the girl, Allison. What do you want to do with her?"

Allison was Feeney's former girlfriend. She had made the mistake of trying to dump him. He had brought her down the basement of the National Uniform Rental Company one night and she had never left. He used her as a fucktoy and to feed and clean the other female prisoners while they awaited shipment. She had been in the basement for about two years and was a shadow of her former voluptuous self. Her neck was connected via a chain to a pipe that ran the length of the basement so that she could slide her long leash up and down it. She had been watching when Jake did the job on Feeney. She had enjoyed watching him beg and plead for his life, offering anything and everything he could think of. She liked Mary

Ellen so far. She hadn't yet beat her. At the present, she was lodged in her own cage, bound and hooded, with plugs in her ears, like all of the imprisoned girls. She was oblivious to Mary Ellen's conversation with Jake.

Jake thought for a moment. "Why can't she keep doing what she's been doing?"

"Taking care of the girls?" Mary Ellen shrugged. "Okay, but when the operation shuts down, somebody's got to do her. She's no good to sell and she knows too much."

"I guess we'll deal with that when the time comes." Jake answered.

It was about 10 o'clock the next morning that Jake got a call from his service. Felix had left a message that a guy was here to see him. Jake called Felix. "Tell him to meet me in the luncheonette down the street. I'll be there in twenty minutes."

When Jake walked into the dingy luncheonette, there was a hard looking man, short, grayish black hair, a determined face, sitting in the last booth. He was drinking coffee. Jake nodded to him and joined him. The waitress came over. Jake ordered coffee. There was a brief silence after she left.

Sergi was a former inmate of the Soviet penal system, and not for political crimes either. You had to have balls to commit real crimes in a police state. He had suffered his knocks and had no fear.

"American coffee sucks," he told Jake.

Jake waited for the waitress to leave his in front of him before answering. "So drink tea."

Sergi laughed. "Your tea sucks too."

"So what about us do you like?" Jake shot back.

"Your women, naked, sucking my cock." Sergi said.

"I understand that there's a two way traffic going on. Lots of Russian whores here too."

The Russian shrugged. "They're all whores," he said. He lifted his coffee cup and took a sip. He was wearing a black, turtle neck sweater and dark brown corduroy pants. There was a large gold ring on his right hand, with an emblem stamped into it. Jake was wearing a light grey t-shirt and jeans.

"Whatever you say," Jake said. "But let's talk about business."

"The price stays the same."

"Okay," Jake answered.

"And no bullshit."

"No bullshit." Jake promised.

"I assume that our former manager told you all the details before he went on his trip?" Sergi asked.

"Correct," Jake answered.

"I'm going to find out all about you," Sergi told Jake.

"Fine," Jake replied. "There is one thing, though."

"Okay. What?"

"My principal is interested in becoming, let's say, an investor overseas. He's looking for a nice place to spend some time, vacation. A place with all the right amenities." Jake explained. "He's willing to make large investments. He has certain outlets for goods that might be convenient to merchants overseas. And he contributes to all the right causes."

The bait was out.

"I'll get back to you," was Sergi's only answer.

* * * * * * * * * * * * * *

After her whipping, Maddy had dedicated herself wholly to her training and the pleasing of her master. During the day, when she was running at the wheel, learning to trot, to canter and to sprint, she was able to forget all about her past. There was only the exhilaration of her body, the sun and the wide open skies. And if she was selected for sex by one of the trainers or foremen on the estate, she let her passions take her away without guilt.

But at night, either tethered in her stall, or brought out to the commons for the amusement of the men, the despair and sorrow of what she had become, of what they had done to her would seep into her. Alone, immobilized for sleep, she would cry bitter tears as she mourned the loss of her voice, her hands, her power to choose.

For if one had to sum up in one phrase all of the miseries and pain that had been inflicted on the poor ponygirl, the former bright, young, happy woman, it would be that her power to choose had been stolen away from her. She could not choose when to eat, to sleep, to defecate. She could not choose when to rest, when to run, when to stand silent and alone. She could not choose the company she kept or who would enter her body. And she could not even choose when to accept pleasure, or to decline pain.

Drabik's campaign to make her learn to reach climax solely through the stimulation of her rear passage was a case in point. It was a practice she had long ago sworn to avoid. But she had lost the power to prevent the invasion of this most private place. It was not enough that her flesh be made subject to her wills of others. Her mind would be forced to accept a new definition of pleasure, a new synapse of sexual excitement. Slowly, but surely, her will would be turned to her masters'.

And she was ready to accept it. Her whipping that day when she had finished the morning race last for the final time had changed her. She knew that she had deserved to be whipped. She also knew that the whipping had spurred her to greater and more successful efforts to please her lord. She ran harder and faster then she ever had before. When she came to understand what her trainer wanted, and now she almost always understood it right away, she began to yearn for it too.

The sexual excitement that she had begun to feel had grown and grown each day and each night, as her rear passage was plowed many times. It became customary, during the lunch break at the middle of the day, for Maddy to kneel on the grass under the large maple tree by the training wheel, her head down, her long legs tucked beneath her, her rear cheeks spread, an invitation to all who walked by. But no matter how hard she tried, no matter how hard she thrust back at the thick cocks that plundered her, no matter how tightly she tried to squeeze the male flesh inside her tight anal ring, she just could not force herself over the top.

It would typically begin with a shouted greeting from one of the men to her trainer. She would not see who it was, her featureless, blue face buried between her knees. The men would converse in their harsh, Slavic tongue. She might smell the smoke from a cigarette. She might hear them laugh. Sometimes the men would stand over her, watching her, their eyes burning into her arched back, her bound wrists.

And then, as the anonymous man knelt down behind her, she would feel his hot, rough hands on her buttocks, caressing them, causing her skin and her pussy to tingle. They would rub their hardening cocks along the valley between her rear cheeks, their hands on the inside of her thighs.

And then the hot tip of the man's prick would probe her still narrow ring, forcing it to widen as the stiff meat entered her bowels. She had learned how to relax her rear muscles, to make her anal ring supple and loose, ready to be impaled. She had learned to love the feeling of a rigid cock as it dragged across the tender flesh of her rear entrance. The fullness of her bowels and the feeling of the hot meat inside her thrilled her. She would sigh and moan as the hard rod began to inflame her. The man's excitement, the sound of his passion, drove her lust higher and higher. She would be panting, yearning for release. And then she would feel the heavy hands that held her shoulders for leverage or which rubbed and stroked her rear globes while thrusting deeply into her, tighten and grab her flesh. The man would grunt and stiffen. She could feel his cock pulse as it drew back and forth over her sphincter. And then he would come, shooting his hot discharge into her bowels. As he withdrew, she would whimper and cry, denied release once more.

During this time, Drabik never touched her. He had the keys to her sealed off loins. He held the keys to her mouth. Her rear was as open to him as it was to any other man. But except for the tug on her leash, the crack of a whip on her hindquarters, there was no contact between them. She was denied the warmth of his flesh, the heat of his rigid manhood.

She knew that he fucked the other ponies. More than once, she watched, kneeling, her golden nose ring leashed to a post, while he used his prick to make some other pony grunt and squeal with pleasure. She watched with envy as she saw their lips encompass him. Her thighs yearned for him, her mouth hungered for him. And she knew that only when she had pleased him, by forcing her body to mold itself to his will, would he deign to press his flesh against hers, to enter her and spill his seed within her.

Finally, ten days after Drabik's cruel regimen had begun, it came. She had been kneeling in the sun, its hot rays caressing her back. It was late afternoon. They had finished her workouts for the day. Drabik was sitting with his back against a tree. She could hear birds singing off in the distance, feel the cooling breeze brush along her back. Her mind began to float. It was as if she had been transported to a new level of being. She could feel every part of her body in unity with the rest, even the useless hands and fingers bound behind her back.

When the man knelt behind her, his contact with her flesh did not disturb her reverie. As he laid his hands on her rear, she could feel her very essence flow into them, become part of them. When his tool pierced the brown rose between her cheeks, she felt her life force flowing back to her there. The friction of the unknown man's member ignited her whole body with sensation. It was as if all the world had slowed to a crawl except the pulses of pleasure that coursed through her. Her mind forgot who and where she was. She was nothing more than the act itself, the energy generated by the teasing of her anal ring.

Suddenly, she felt the lust within her surge. She felt a river of electrified sensation flow like a torrent from her distended and filled bowels to the nerves of her oozing loins. And then it came, a pounding, maddening throbbing deep inside her imprisoned slit. The pleasure jolted through her. She cried out as her body shuddered. As if from a dream, her mind woke up and she felt the rasping of the man's rigid tool across the tender membranes of her rear portal. She squeezed it tightly with her muscles, making exquisite the sensation of it leaving and entering her.

Drabik sat up as he heard his pony cry and moan. She had done it. She had rewired her paths of pleasure by sheer will, a will prompted by the need for obedience, to make her masters' will her own.

When the man had spent his juices inside her, and retreated from her bowels, Maddy gave out a huge sigh. She could feel her heart beating wildly inside her. Her cunt still gave off little spasms of pleasure. It was as if by magic the sensations of her narrow passage had transferred themselves to her soaked pussy. For her, ass fucking would never be the same.

Drabik snapped his fingers sharply. Maddy automatically rose to her knees. Sweat gleamed on her body; her chest was painted red with evidence of her spent lust. Her breasts rose and fell with her chest, quivering seductively. Drabik snapped his fingers again and Maddy came to him. Kneeling in front of him, she watched him unbutton his fly. His thickening cock spilled out. He beckoned the pony towards him and motioned for her to lower her head. He produced a key and loosened the locks that held her bit in her mouth.

Maddy felt joy at the prospect that her master would enter her, that she had earned the chance to pleasure him. He pulled her hooded head to his loins. She seized his stiff prick with her mouth, running her tongue over its tip, pressing her lips down his shaft. As Drabik's body absorbed the soothing sensation of the ponygirl's warm mouth, his eyes took in the delicate curves of her hips, the beautiful soft skin of her rear. Her long, auburn ponytail laid spread across her back, her bound hands were held wide open as if waiting to receive his gift.

The ponygirl was delirious with pleasure as her master's hardness passed across her trembling lips. She felt him place his hands gently on her head and guide her down until she had engulfed him fully. Slowly and steadily he raised and lowered her head to satisfy his desires. Maddy, bent over, her knees beneath her, let his desires be hers. She willed herself to be the instrument of his self pleasure. She ran her tongue around his cock's plump end as he drew her head up, and slid it the length of his shaft as he pushed her down. She felt like the whole world was in her mouth, filling her being.

Drabik luxuriated in the feel of Maddy's tongue and lips. His heat began to rise, his eyes rolled back. He loved this faceless pony's mouth. He had denied it to himself while he waited for her to succumb, but now he reveled in it, and, finally allowed himself to discharge in it. His orgasm poured a steady cascade of pleasure throughout his body.

He let Maddy continue to caress his softening manhood. She had taken every drop of his seed, moaning her joy at its receipt.

For a few moments, Drabik sat there, his mind and body floating. He casually caressed Maddy's hooded head as she held his now limp meat within her mouth. Then, remembering his duty to his employer, he pulled the ponygirl's head from his loins and restored her bit, locking it in place. He pulled her to her feet by the ring of her collar. He leashed her and pulled her after him towards the barn. She expected to go to her stall to wash up and eat, but he led her to the common area where the other trainers were loitering, getting ready to go to the bunkhouse for dinner. Holding her leash with one hand, he wheeled out the cart on which she had been confined once before.

Maddy's heart dropped as she realized that her rear portal was to be made convenient for the cocks of the other men. Her moment of communion with her master was over. She would continue to serve his will, but without his presence.

After Drabik had secured Maddy to the cart, her body bent over, her rear accessible to all, he left.

She did not see him again until the next day. Her ass was used through the night by the men as it pleased them. Each time, her mind would become beclouded with passion as she felt her rear passage filled. She came again and again for the men, gurgling out her pleasure from behind the bit that pressed down on her tongue.

In the morning, Maddy was led to the training wheel in the usual way. She had hoped that her master would remove the cage around her loins. He did not, and for the next three days, like before, he continued to proffer her rear to passersby. Only now she would cry and moan with passion as she was led repeatedly to orgasm. He did not deign to enjoy her himself.

Maddy's sex began to yearn for her master's prick. At night, bound and chained, her mind would center on her unused slit and its emptiness. As she came again and again, bent over, receiving one hard prick after another in her bowels, she would feel her cunt's anguished need, a cunt that her master controlled.

On the evening of the third day, after her dinner was done, she was chained in her stall, her legs spread wide, her belly against the pole that bisected it, a chain connecting her golden nose ring to the wall in front of her, when she heard the door open behind her. She had been standing with her eyes closed, trying to assuage the aching need of her empty sex. She felt hands undoing her ankles from their confinements. She saw her trainer dip under the rail at her hips and loosen the leash that connected her nose ring to the wall. He led her outside, away from the barn. There was a large, freshly mowed lawn there and he brought her to her knees and then laid her down on her back, her bound arms behind her digging into the loose grass. Looking up, she could see through the tiny holes in her hood a small section of night sky, the twinkling of stars in the crystal clear air. Drabik lay down beside the faceless, blue hooded pony, and took her nipple in his mouth, kissing it softly. His hand roamed across her chest and seized the other breast and began to massage it gently. Maddy felt her need rising. She spread her legs and dug her heels into the grass in hopeful anticipation of her use. She felt his hot hands descend her torso down to her waist. The chains that had held her hot slit prisoner so long were loosened and removed from her belt. She felt his hand lift the narrow metal cup from her sex. Her sheath began to flow with her lubricating juices; she thrust her hips up invitingly.

Drabik separated himself from the supine pony and drew off his clothes. He rolled over her leg and placed himself between Maddy's spread, white thighs. Her skin seemed to glow in the moonlight. Her dark nipples were hard and seemed to float over her pearl white breasts. The rampant wolf tattooed on her belly undulated as her taut muscles tensed at his touch. Slowly, he crept forward until his cock stood poised over her soft, heat filled gate. When he plunged within, Maddy gave a muffled cry. Her hungry nether mouth sucked his manhood in. She was delirious with joy. Drabik drove long, deep thrusts into her that pushed her lust higher and higher. She came with a mighty moan as she felt him spill within her, her hips jammed against his, her booted feet curled around his thighs pulling him deeper and deeper inside.

They lay entwined for several minutes. Maddy treasured the feel of his body against the length of hers. When his softening cock slipped free, he rolled off of her, but lay pressed up to her side, exchanging his heat with hers, his hand languidly caressing her breasts. When he felt her nipples harden again, he dragged his calloused fingers down her taut belly and then brought her off by hand.

* * * * * * * * * * * * * * *

It is hot in May in Kalikastan. Cold in winter, hot as hell in summer. The racing season was short. Six weeks in the spring. And in the fall, another six. In May, the fillies acquired in March and April were barely getting their legs together, but there were races for the 'yearlings' as they were called. Small purses, but exciting to watch. There was always some talent to take note of, ponies that would be real challengers at the next meeting.

Maddy had been taken in the beginning of March. By the first week in April she was ready to be hitched to a team. After the morning race and her breakfast routines, Maddy was led by Drabik back to the track. She knew nothing of his plans, of course, because she didn't need to.

She was surprised when they headed up the path to the track instead of going to the training wheel. When they reached it she saw a small carriage sitting there. Already in the traces was a dark skinned pony with a thick, black mane rising out of her tight blue hood. Although, like Maddy, her face was covered and featureless, she seemed older than most of the ponies, yet her breasts were still high and firm, her legs lean and well muscled.

Now, it would have been much easier to sit down and explain to Maddy what she had to do. But that was contraindicated according to all experienced pony trainers. If someone started talking to her, she might begin to believe that she was a woman again, that she was an equal to her masters. No, it was better that she learn on the job, so to speak. It would take patience, the liberal but judicious use of a whip and the help of another pony.

Jezebel was one of the oldest and most experienced ponies on the estate. She was not sure how long she had been a pony, five or six summers, as she measured time, maybe more. She had run with every kind of rig they had there, the small two wheeled traps, the two pony cabriolet, the landau, a large formal carriage pulled by nine ponygirls and, of course, the formula one carriage of pony racing, the sulky, used in harness racing all over the world. The estate also had a troika, requiring the service of three ponies, a barouche, a four wheeled carriage with two double seats, and a four ponied post chaise.

Maddy's first pull was to be a trap, a small, light, two wheeled pony cart. For training purposes it was set up for two ponies. Once ponies became skilled enough and strong enough, they sometimes pulled one rider in a trap by themselves. But today was for the purposes of getting Maddy acclimated to her new tasks and to refine her skills on the reins.

Drabik had worked with Maddy for the last week using long reins attached to her bridle. To Maddy, it was merely another method of control. She was losing the ability to think ahead and so she did not connect the use of the reins with anything else. Of course, she had seen daily the other ponies pulling carriages and carts along the roads and tracks, but her status as a new pony in training insulated her from feeling connected to what the other ponies did.

Trainers were not drivers, per se, and a lean looking youth sat smiling on the small seat of the rig. He hopped out and brought over a leather harness. Maddy, for a moment, became dizzy. She had been running, training for several weeks. She had forgotten what for. She was now confronted with the physical evidence of her new, real purpose in life. She trembled as the leather accouterment was added to her body. Thick leather straps went over her shoulders and around her waist. They were connected by two broad straps that went above and below the breasts in the front and in comparable locations across the back. A strap descended from the strap above her breasts to the one below through the space between her generous breasts. Her naked orbs seemed more pronounced, framed by the coarse leather. Since there would be a plethora of straps and ropes around her as she hauled the carriage, leather mittens were placed over her hands so that her fingers would not catch on anything.

The frightened pony had to be coaxed between the shafts. Her knees felt week and her heart was pounding. Her despair at the loss of her personhood returned. She had become an animal, she thought miserably. Here was the ultimate proof.

Up to now, Maddy had considered her new life as some sort of horrible costume drama, a costume nightmare, really, assuaged only by her dedication to he who she thought of as her master. But now she was confronted with a utilitarian justification for her training and her servile condition. She looked desperately for Drabik as she was hitched in place. She saw him walking down the pathway back to the barn. The driver turned her head so that he could apply the reins to her bridle.

Once the reins were attached, the other end tied off to a hitch on the cart, there was really no place to look but straight ahead. The tension on the reins was transferred through the bridle to the bit, which caused the metal plate on the bit to depress on her tongue. That caused first discomfort and then, if more pressure was maintained, nausea and pain. With the reins tied off on the carriage, any sideways movement of the head caused the bridle to pull on one side, which, in turn, caused the plate to depress on one part of her mouth. When Maddy tried to turn to watch her trainer disappear, she winced in pain and quickly turned back.

The young man was gentle and made low, comforting sounds as he tightened the cinches on her harness. There were three shafts in front of the cart. One was connected to the right side of Maddy's harness by the waist. There was a ring in the shaft and the driver looped a belt on the side of the harness through it. The shaft rode up almost directly on Maddy's hip. There would be as little play as possible so that every forward motion would be transferred immediately and directly to the cart behind her. Maddy's training pony, Jezebel, was tied to the middle shaft in a similar manner, but on her opposite hip. The ponies were separated from each other by only the width of the shaft. The outside shafts were similarly attached to their outside hips.

Thick straps with clips on the end led from the bottom of the cart to three points on the back of Maddy's belt. Another long strap ran to the middle of her back and affixed to a belt connecting the two horizontal straps. Once the clips were on, the driver cinched them tight. Maddy would be able to exert force on the cart from six places, her hips, the middle of her back, which drew strength from her shoulders, and the three straps connected to her belt in the rear. It was designed so that the strain of pulling would be distributed as evenly as possible throughout the body.

Maddy's feeling of despair grew with the tightening of each belt around her. The sensation of unreality that struck her when she first found herself shaved and outfitted as a ponygirl came back to her now. She could see the hard dirt track ahead of her curving to her left several hundred yards away, the white rail fencing, the golden fields beyond, but nothing else. Her world was reduced to what she could see through the little dime sized holes in her hood and by the limitations of the movement of her head. She could sense, but could not turn her head to see, the ponygirl next to her.

When the blond haired driver had Maddy all hitched up, he came in front of her. He patted her on the head and caressed her beasts, pulling on the nipples until they were hard. He ran his hands over her hips and down her legs. He placed one hand on her naked, hairless mons, and dragged his fingers up and down the slit between her labial lips causing the disks that hung there to jingle, until he felt her begin to lubricate. Maddy realized that what the young boy was doing was claiming her. He was showing her that he controlled her, that he determined what she felt and experienced. When he was done, after she had moaned with growing passion, he patted the side of her hooded face and went back to the carriage. The desperately frightened pony felt the sensation of him climbing aboard through her straps and the shafts hooked to her sides. She was crying as she realized that she was about to take the first steps of thousands, maybe millions, that she would take as a servile beast.

Maddy felt the straps to her bridle tighten slightly as the driver took them in his hands. She felt a soft tug on them as if to get her attention and then the universal "tschk, tschk," from the man's mouth, signaling his ponies to go.

The shaft next to Maddy pulled forward as the pony to her right responded to the signal. She started too. Her mind and body were trained to commands. When she moved forward, she felt the weight of the cart and driver on her body. It was surprisingly light. She tried to match her pace to her neighbor's. Another line had been crossed in her dehumanization.

The driver had started them out really slow, just a walking pace. By the time they had made one trip around the track, the cart seemed to be getting heavier. On the end of the second circuit, it was heavier still, and so on. The driver had them circle the track ten times before they stopped. Maddy was glad for the break. It had been hard, but not overwhelmingly so. She tried to envision what she looked like as she hauled the cart around. Since her vision was so limited, she felt as if the whole world was watching her.

The driver gave the ponies a five minute break. He had a plastic bottle of water with a long, thin neck, and he was able to give them water by loosening the bridal and pouring it over the bit. He gave them just a taste, enough to water their mouths. He tightened the bridles and resumed his place on the single seat trap. Maddy heard the signal to start and felt the slight tug on the reins again.

After about a quarter mile, she felt the reins jump again. She recognized this signal from her training with Drabik. It meant to trot. Her legs were slightly heavy from walking the small carriage around the track, but she complied automatically. At first, she was comfortable with the pace.

It felt strange to have her breasts flowing up and down on her chest while the rest of her upper torso was so tightly confined. After the first lap around the 1500 meter track, however, the pace began to tell on her. When she started to slow down, she felt the sting of a pony whip on her rear. It made a 'crack!' as it struck her, and it hurt. She forced her self to keep up the pace. At the far turn, her legs started to become as heavy as lead. Her chest heaved in the search for oxygen. This was nothing like running around the training wheel. The burden of the slender boy and the mechanical contraption on which he sat, even though it was shared between her and Jezebel, felt like it doubled her weight. She started to slow down again and 'crack!' the whip struck her again. A wave of misery flowed through her. Is this what her life was going to be like, she thought as the aches in her legs and thighs began to become burns.

When they completed the lap, Maddy had hoped that the boy would let her rest. After all, it was only her first day. As if he were reading her mind, 'crack!' came another fierce bite from the whip.

Maddy began to wail and sob as she forced herself to maintain the punishing pace. She began to stumble, and each time that she did she received another fierce bite on her haunches. When they reached the end of the third lap, the boy brought them to a halt. The pressure of the bit in her mouth as he pulled back on the reins, pushing her tongue down and almost into her throat, made Maddy's stomach churn. It was an effective signal to stop.

The pony's chest heaved for breath. Her body sagged. She gulped down the water the boy gave her. She felt him get back into the cart. Her heart was heavy with misery as she awaited the signal to move. But the boy waited. She heard the striking of a match and then smelled the unmistakable scent of burning tobacco. She could even see the blue gray smoke as it wafted in front of her.

Waiting was part of a pony's duties too.

When the boy felt they had rested enough, he stepped out of the cart and went in front of them. He lowered the flaps over the eyes on Maddy's hood. She was startled. How could she run if she were blind? But ponies were not supposed to decide which way to go. That was up to the driver. On a flat track she didn't need her sight at all. The driver would guide her through the delicate use of the reins. A pull on the left one meant to go left; a pull on the right to go right. Simple.

Again, the driver had them walk ten laps around the track. It was a strange experience and Maddy had to be encouraged several times with the whip to continue to move. Since she couldn't see, her mind concentrated fully on the strain on her torso and legs as she and her companion hauled the two wheeled carriage around the track. Blind as she was, she had no idea how many times they had lapped it, nor, of course, how many the boy intended for them to do. When they rounded the turns of the track, she felt a gentle pulling on her left. It was mild and so she altered her gait slightly. When the pressure lifted, she turned straight again.

She was exhausted when they finally stopped. The boy left the blinders on. She felt the neck of the water bottle in her mouth and she swallowed it greedily. She hoped and prayed that her ordeal for the day would be over, but after a few minutes, she felt the boy get back into the cart and the flick of the reins that signaled to go. When it flicked again to begin to trot, her mind began to overflow with fear. She knew how tired her legs were, how her energy had been sapped by the prior runs. She knew what would happen if she failed.

Running with the flaps down on her eyeholes was like running in a darkened room. There was a quarter inch gap between the inside of the hood and the surface of her eye. Nothing was holding her eyelid down like a blindfold would do. She ran with her eyes open, literally looking into darkness. It was if she had been thrust into another dimension where light didn't exist, running and running and going nowhere.

Maddy got just past the first turn when her legs began to feel like they were trapped in viscous, hardening cement. It became agony to lift them, to push down on the clay surface. But each time she tried to ease the pace, to catch her breath, she would feel the sharp sting on her rear. She continued to run, sobbing and crying, wishing for death, for liberation from her dismal life. Her trainer had turned from her, handed her off. Who would care for her now? "Maybe if I just stop," she thought desperately. "I'll stop and refuse to go on! I'll take the whippings, the beatings, but I won't run a single step further!" Just as that thought finished crossing her mind, she felt another bite of the whip, cried out, and increased her pace. She knew then that she would run as long as they wanted her to, as long as her body held out.

It came on her all at once. Suddenly, her body could go no further, it gave out. She fell in the traces, her legs dragging along the packed, dirt surface. She felt the bit lean hard against her tongue as she fell, and the pain struck her like a blow to the head. The boy pulled back on the reins, causing Maddy further pain and anguish. The cart stopped and the boy jumped out.

Maddy felt the burning of the lash as it struck her body
again and again. She cried out for mercy, in her darkness.
She tried to stand, but her legs felt like rubber. The lash
brought lines of fire across her legs, her shoulders, her
breasts. Finally, using all of her strength, she pushed her
body up with her legs. When she was standing, the lashing
stopped.

The unhappy pony cried and moaned. "Why am I
here?" she wailed in her mind. "Why me? Why? What did
I ever do?" She could feel her tears soaking her hood.
When the boy regained his seat in the cart, the reins flicked
and she began to walk. Soon they were up to trotting speed
again, and within a few minutes, Maddy had fallen again.
Five times in all she fell that day, and five times she was
beaten until she stood.

Finally, the boy brought them to a halt for the day.
Maddy's body felt as limp as a rag. She had descended to a
place that she didn't even know existed. "Could this be
worse than death?" she thought miserably.

Her blinders still on, Maddy was removed from the
traces. She felt the harness and the gloves from her hands
removed. The boy was slender, but strong and she felt him
half carry her by her arm until they reached a tall, one foot
round pole stuck in the ground just outside of the track.
She felt her body turned around and her back pressed
against the pole. The back of her collar was fastened to it
and a strap run around her waist, holding her tightly bound
there. Another went around her ankles.

Maddy realized that she was to be beaten for her
failures. She cried and moaned and tried to gurgle pleas for
mercy out through her bit. The first blow, from a two inch
round hickory cane, struck her right across the breasts. She
howled in pain. Since they would be needing her thighs

again tomorrow, there was no sense beating them. But the breasts served no function as she ran. Maddy received, in all, five painful bruising blows across her breasts, one for each fall. She had been whipped before, but had never felt the dull but intense pain caused by a blow from a cane. The pain seemed to sink inside of her, bruising her inner self. After the fifth blow, she just sagged, blubbering in pain, moaning for pity.

The boy released her from the post and let her fall to the ground. Maddy curled up into a ball in her misery.

She did not know how long she lay there. After a long while, she felt strong arms grab her by the upper arms and lift her up. When she was steady on her feet, she felt a leash attach to her collar. She followed the unknown man's lead docilely.

When they reached the barn, her bridle was removed and replaced with her gag. Her eye flaps were lifted and she could see again. She was in the common area of the barn and a large wooden table with a pad on it had been set up. At first she thought that she was to be laid out on it and beaten again. But gentle hands encouraged her to lie down on it on her stomach. Her wrists were loosened from her back and affixed to a ring at the top of the table. Straps held her ankles in place. And then hands laid themselves on her, strong, knowledgeable hands. A soothing, almost burning ointment was applied to the back of her thighs and to her calves and the hands slowly, firmly rubbed it in. The contrast to the whipping she had just received could not have been greater. Her muscles seemed to sigh with relief as the hands worked them. Maddy's eyes were turned to the wall and she could not see who was performing this pleasurable service for her. She didn't care. He did her back too, touching regions that had been hidden by her bound wrists. When her back was finished, she was turned over, and the front of her thighs received the same warm, comforting attention. A cool cloth was applied to her breasts, and the throbbing of her bruised globes began to diminish.

Maddy was allowed to lay in her stall for the rest of the day. Every hour or so, someone would come and get her and make her walk around the inside of the barn for a while. She was fed a clear broth. Maddy did what was required, she ate what they gave her, but her heart had been cruelly damaged. Her master had abandoned her. She had been nothing to him. Just a beast to be trained. As she lay on her pallet in her stall, her legs strapped together, her neck and ankle bound to rings in the floor, her eyes sealed off from the world, she felt empty, drained. Tomorrow, she knew, she would have to run in the traces again. This time she would know in advance what pain failure would bring. She was sure her breasts would be black and blue tomorrow. But what did it matter anyway. Let them kill her, she thought.

It was late, around ten o'clock. Maddy was being led around the barn one last time for the day, to prevent her muscles from cramping up. The other ponies, except for one or two who were being used by trainers, were in their stalls. She followed the lead that was affixed to her collar forlornly.

When they returned to her stall, there was someone inside it. It was her trainer, her master. He took the leash from the stable boy and pulled her inside. Maddy started to cry. She could not stand the thought of his abandonment of her. Had he come there to prove his mastery over her? To taunt her? She had no power to make him go away, or to refuse anything to him. Or to anyone for that matter. Her body yearned for him, and she feared his indifference.

Drabik looked at the damaged breasts of the ponygirl. He had expected as much. The drivers had no time for subtlety with their charges. He knew how she would be feeling after her first day in harness. He had come to sooth her, to reward her for her suffering.

He backed Maddy up to the rail that ran across her stall. Leaving her there he retrieved the special board made to lay the pony on over it. After putting it in place, he lifted her up onto the rail. He leaned Maddy back and strapped her torso to it. He then pulled her legs up, spreading them wide and fixing her ankles to the rail. Her loins lay open to him. He ran his hands down her thighs and over her belly. He cupped her aching breasts and kissed each nipple delicately.

When Maddy felt the hands of her master caress her she felt a wave of relief pass through her. These were not the hands of indifference. She knew then that although he had passed her into the hands of others that he would still be near, that she would see him and that he would visit her. That no matter who commanded her or used her, it would always be him that she served.

The touch of her master's hands electrified Maddy's body. She yearned for him to enter her, to find his pleasure inside her. Her pussy swelled in invitation to him, her nipples hardened in adoration of his touch.

Drabik moved his lips from Maddy's tortured breasts and ran his mouth across her belly. His hot lips drank in her skin. She felt him kiss her thighs, run his tongue along the sides of her engorged nether lips. And then she felt it trace the lines of her dilating slit. She sighed deeply in pleasure. His tongue teased her clit and then his lips descended on it sucking soothingly, drawing her blood to it.

All her doubts and fears fell away as she felt her lust build. She moaned as he sank his hot tongue deeply inside her, stroking the lining of her sheath, making her swoon.

Drabik drank in Maddy's lustful aroma as her juices flowed freely from within her. She began to move her hips, to try and stroke her cunt on his tongue. He placed his hands on her thighs, spreading them wider, immobilizing her. She would take her pleasure in his time, as he willed it. He pulled his lips free of her soft, wet tunnel and let her moan in frustration. Her chest was heaving, causing her wounded breasts to shiver and sway. He let her moan again, and then he returned his lips to her widened labia, his tongue to her crevasse. He kept her on the verge of passionate release for a long time. She moaned and cried, her mind begging for completion. He sucked on her clit, pulling it to its length, stretching the skin around it. And then he ran the tip of tongue along its top, flicking it delicately. He would let her come now. Her felt her hips struggle against his hands, her torso shudder. Her voice was one long, low moan. When her pussy began to contract and spasm, he drove his tongue deep within her and began to lick the length of her slit, lingering on her hardened bud of pleasure. Her body shook and convulsed as her orgasm tore threw her. Her pussy muscles clasped tightly, repeatedly, like a fist opening and closing. She arched her back as the pleasure flowed through her.

Maddy was still in the waning throes of her orgasm when Drabik drew his stiff cock from his pants. He drove it deep into her pussy, releasing another torrent of pleasure from her loins. Her cunt was fiery hot, her juices flowing out of her. When he had covered his cock with her juices, he withdrew and presented it to her delicate rear star. Maddy gasped as Drabik's meat passed freely in. He had not used her narrow portal since she had rewired herself for him and the young, passionate ponygirl was overcome with joy that he had entered her there. She groaned and cried out as she came again, reveling in the feel of his hard staff teasing the sensitive tissue of her little ring. When he came, her mind went blank, all of her consciousness flowing to where he possessed her.

Drabik withdrew from the panting, moaning pony. Her skin was mottled with the signs of her passion. Her pussy leaked her discharge. After returning his tool to its home, he placed a tender kiss on Maddy's yawning sex and then left her to enjoy her silent reverie.

The next week was tortuous for Maddy. The blond haired boy drove her mercilessly. He whipped her cruelly when she fell, and gave her the equivalent number of strong strokes from the cane on various parts of body at the end of each session. She began to think of it as the price for ending the day. Drabik did not come to her again until the third night, when her pushed her to her knees and allowed her to suck his cock to orgasm. She missed her trainer's daily attentions, but was comforted with the knowledge that he had not forgotten her.

She continued to be used by the other men on a regular basis. She spread her thighs for them when ordered, opened her mouth at their command to receive their conscienceless pricks, presented her rear portal for penetration. She was powerless to prevent her own lust rising as one or another, or sometimes two at once drove into her. She cried out and moaned when she came, her sexual appetite almost insatiable. This was in keeping with the well accepted principle that it was necessary to maintain total physical and mental dominance over the pony. On days when a particular pony had not received use, it was the duty of the stable boys to take up the slack. On many nights Maddy could hear the moans and cries of other ponies as they were stroked or fucked to orgasm before being put to bed.

But the blond driver had never used her. Each time, after he beat her, he led Jezebel away and left her lying there desolately in the dust. Jezebel was not housed in the same barn as Maddy. Maddy's barn was for the training of racing ponies. Jezebel had done her turn as a racer, but now, along with seven other older ponies, served Axil Grobgy, the gangster cum country gentleman, and the owner of the vast estate, as general purpose ponies. Grobgy or his beautiful amoral daughter, Anya, would use them to visit neighboring estates or for picnics or leisurely perambulations through the countryside. Guests were often entertained by taking them for a spin.

Not all of the more than thirty ponies in Maddy's barn would be kept by Grobgy for his racing stable. Some would just not meet the high standards that he set for his racing ponies. These would be sold to lesser lights in the Kalikastan criminal pantheon for personal use or for their own racing stables. Some prospered by being in the hands of new trainers and became real competitors on the circuit. Others just served as status symbols. Anyone who was anyone in Kalikastan wanted a racing pony.

Each day Maddy got stronger and stronger. Finally, on the tenth day, she managed to complete her training session for the first time without falling. At the end of the day, when her harness was removed, the blond boy patted her on the head, smiling. He pressed her to her knees in the dust and proffered her his limp cock. Maddy began to cry as she seized it with her lips and felt it grow hard in her mouth. She sucked on it fervently, eagerly bringing pleasure to her tormentor. She knew that he was rewarding her, and, in spite of the fact that she was repelled by and feared this cruel boy who had beat her unmercifully for days on end, she considered herself blessed that he found her mouth suitable. She was grateful, and it seemed blissful, to have her tormentor's manhood between her lips rather than his cane at her breasts. She caressed him passionately, pressing his cock deep within her. He shuddered and groaned as he came, spilling his seed in her throat.

CHAPTER FIVE

A few days later, Jezebel was replaced by a younger pony. Unbeknownst to Maddy, while she had been training every morning for hours on end, this pony, another yearling like Maddy, had been training in the afternoons. She was a long tailed blond, almost a twin of Maddy in bodily proportions. She was called Persephone, although her former name had been Paula Stewart. She had been an art student at the University of Maryland. She was invited by a Russian exchange program to study a collection of fourteenth century icons. She had traveled to a small Ukrainian city called Dianstana, outside of Odessa, where she was to be taken to the remote monastery where the icons were housed. She was never heard from again.

There were two training sessions now, one in the morning and one in the afternoon, and the matched pair became faster and faster. A week after they had been paired, when they had been brought to the track for their morning session, a short, slender man wearing a beret and tight white pants tucked into high, black boots was waiting for them. He wore a well trimmed goatee. Alongside him were the young blond driver, Drabik, another man, who had been Persephone's trainer, Axil Grobgy and his daughter Anya. Maddy had not seen Drabik for over a week and she felt a chill go through her as she was led by a stable boy to where the people were standing. She still yearned for his touch and the sight of him made her suffer from his apparent indifference.

Grobgy was the fist to speak as the two ponies were presented to the bereted man. "Here they are Vadym, what do you think?"

Maddy recognized the speaker as the man who had been the first to rape her on the day she arrived. She remembered the swarthy face and the broad, thick black mustache. He had grinned as he made her come with his cock before a crowd of his workers as she lay splayed over a bale of hay. She had not thought of him much since the day he had watched Drabik work her at the training wheel. As Maddy recalled his hard, cruel face, she remembered that he was her owner. She was his property as much as any dog or horse on his estate. Fear passed through her as she looked at him.

She also remembered the slender, stylish and beautiful young woman at his side. She had a full head of long, black hair and her skin was smooth and white. The woman had asked her trainer to let her watch her orgasm and Drabik had made Maddy, a newly dehumanized pony, stand before her, her legs spread, while he fingered her to pleasure from behind. She had been shamed then, as the lady watched her body shake and quiver as she obediently orgasmed. And she was shamed now to stand naked in front of her. It had been many weeks since she had been conscious of her nudity, her shaven nether lips, her exposed breasts. She had almost forgotten that there existed real women who wore clothes and laughed and spoke. Her sense of herself as a simulacrum of a woman had never been so intense. She shared bodily traits with this human being, but nothing else.

But what astounded Maddy the most was her face. It wasn't any particular thing about it. It was the fact that she had one. Her single glance at this woman told her more about her than she knew about any of the ponies she had spent weeks with. She looked self satisfied. Her eyes bespoke a streak of cruelty. She was alert and poised. All this she could tell from one glance. That is what a face did for you, it gave you personality. All of hers had been taken away.

Vadym looked over the two hooded ponygirls. He advanced to Maddy, apparently disinterested in her breasts or her exposed sex. He placed his hands on her thighs, squeezing them tightly. He ran his hand down the inside of her legs, testing the muscles. He turned her around, and explored her shoulders and hips. He then did the same thing to Persephone. Seemingly satisfied, he looked back at Maddy's owner and spoke in words unintelligible to either of the unhappy creatures. Whatever was happening here, it bespoke change. For helpless, servile beasts, change was always frightening.

"Okay," he said. "Let's see what they can do."

Vadym was a ponygirl jockey by profession. He had driven the best ponies in the country for the last ten years, since the reintroduction of the sport. If he liked what he saw, he would agree to drive these two, young ponies in the impending racing season. The first match was only ten days away.

Drabik sensed the uncertainty and fear in his former charge. He had been avoiding her. Their time together was finished. He was already working on a new Australian pony that he was training for another estate. She and her friends had been on vacation to Greece. They had gone to a party in the countryside outside Athens. A man had invited them all to fly to his small Aegean island on his private plane. Once there, Doris Lapham and her three friends caught another flight to Kalikastan. Doris was the tallest and the sturdiest of the group. Her other friends were still at Khalid's awaiting masters.

In spite of his disassociation with Maddy, it was traditional for the trainer to be present when a new pony was being looked over by a potential racing driver. He could answer any questions about her training. That explained why he was there. But it didn't explain his touch of pity for the frightened animal. And it didn't explain why he had been purposefully avoiding her. He resisted the urge to step over and reassure her by caressing her breasts or patting her on the head.

The blond driver signaled the stable boys to harness the fillies and put them in their traces. The small cart that they had been pulling was already there and Maddy stood morosely as she was strapped into her leather. When she was fully hitched, the blond boy stood in front of the two nervous ponies and showed them the cane. His meaning was instantly clear.

Maddy was torn between doing her best to impress this new man or to hold back. In her mind, there was only one explanation for what was happening. She believed that the man was looking to buy them. A matched pair. Her stomach turned as the boy mounted the cart and flicked the reins. She dutifully started a slow trot to the track.

The blond boy led them around the track at a slow pace three times. The people had gathered at the track rail and were watching the ponies warm up. Maddy could only catch a small glimpse of them as she passed by. She no longer ran with her eye flaps down. She had proven herself responsive to the driver's handling and now, being more sure footed, could take advantage of her restored sight to build up her speed.

Drabik watched as his protégé displayed her accomplished form. She had taken well to the harness, as he knew she would. He believed that she was destined for great things. Anya disturbed his reminiscences.

"She looks fine, Anton. Don't worry."

He looked at her. "I'm not worried," he responded.

"Do you miss her hot cunt? Why don't you fuck her when we're done. I'd like to watch."

Drabik looked at her with disdain. "Have one of the stable boys do it," he said, annoyed.

"Why are you so touchy, Anton? She's just a pony. We've got more than three dozen of them. Did this one enchant you?"

Drabik wondered about that for a moment. Had she enchanted him?

"Don't be stupid, Anya. I've trained over forty ponies and she is just like all the rest." Was that what he really believed, he thought. He tried to shake off his doubts.

"I tell you what, Anya," he told the sultry young woman, "I'll have one of the stable boys fuck her and then I'll whip her for you. She probably hasn't had a good whipping for a while. And if Vadym likes her, she'll be in his care for the next six weeks. You won't be able to get at her until July."

"That sounds fine to me, Anton. And then will you fuck me? I've missed you. I'll be all hot. Take me to the inn and fuck my brains out!"

Drabik laughed. "For you, I'll do this. But if your father finds out, he'll kill me."

Anya put her hand to Drabik's scarred cheek. "I'll protect you baby. Don't worry."

Maddy and Persephone had warmed up by now. Vadym had watched them carefully, looking for their rhythm, their spirit. Matched pairs needed to be highly coordinated with each other, almost like mirrored images in motion. The standard race for yearlings was the 1500 meters. Vadym walked down to the starting line to observe how well they got off the mark. A few seconds advantage at the beginning of a race could mean a lot. The ponies had practiced starting many times and suffered many blows for their failures. But they now were good at it and Vadym was impressed as the ponies dug their toes deeply into the track's hard packed surface in unison and sprung into motion.

Maddy had decided, as apparently Persephone had too, that there was no percentage in dogging it. Not only that, but warming up had stoked their natural competitiveness and they were eager to show what they could do.

Ponygirls move slower than horses, especially when they are towing a 150 lb. cart and a 175 lb. man. To the uninitiated, their pace may have seemed even torpid. But to Vadym and the others, they were making good time. The blond boy was yelling encouragement to them and cracking the whip as their legs churned up the dirt, a trail of dust following behind them. By the first turn they had reached full sprint and they were maintaining their pace along the back rail. Drabik watched with admiration as the ponies came around the near turn and into the stretch. When they crossed the finish line, they were still maintaining their top speed, a tribute to their durability and strength.

Vadym looked at his stop watch. He curled his lower lip and nodded. "Not bad," he said. "With a little work…, okay. I'll do it."

Grobgy beamed and slapped him on the back. "Good! Good! With a good pair of yearlings we'll have a shot at some top prizes. Everyone, come up to the house for a drink!"

Anya grabbed Drabik's arm. "Don't forget our date," she whispered. "Two drinks and let's get out of there."

Drabik nodded his assent.

Grobgy's house was set on a small rise that dominated the otherwise flat terrain of the estate. It was built in a grand style, befitting his wealth. There was a large, wood paneled foyer and a broad set of marble stairs that led to the upper floors. The rapaciousness of the crime leader did not limit itself to ponygirls, and his house was well staffed with the more mundane variety of female slave. His current count was twenty beautiful young women under his thrall. When not fucking or beating them, he used them as decoration throughout the household or leant them out to his men or his guests.

The group went into what Grobgy called the library because it had a few books in it. Two naked young women were kneeling on either side of the huge fireplace that dominated the room. Their fear showed in their eyes as he passed by them. A tall, lean servant, dressed in a peasant's shirt and loose black pants took their drink orders.

"So, how do you think we'll do this year Anton?" he asked the ponygirl trainer. Anton doubled as one of Grobgy's enforcers. Training ponygirls was a sideline as much as racing them was a sideline to Grobgy. But gentlemen are judged by their hobbies.

"Very well. We've got the 1500 and the 3000 meter sulky down pat. We're a little weak in the four pony divisions, but we're competitive in the troika. If the yearlings hold up we should do okay."

Persephone's trainer spoke up. "I think we'll take the phaeton heats, easy."

Grobgy was pleased. He offered Vadym the use of one of his slave girls, which he graciously accepted. She meekly followed him from the room. Drabik finished his drink and made his apologies. Anya walked out with him. "I'll see you in the tackle room in about fifteen minutes," she said, winking.

Drabik trudged back down to the ponygirl barn. He didn't know why he had agreed to Anya's demands about Maddy, or "Lightning', as he knew her. But he couldn't back out of it now. Besides, he needed to destroy the illusion of any emotional connection between him and the pony. It was bad for her and it was bad for him.

It would have been a great surprise to Maddy to know that her name was left behind at Khalid's when she had been delivered there from the States. Grobgy and Drabik had seen her picture before, with her face blocked out; her name was of no interest to them. To them, she was 'Lightning' and nothing else.

The ponygirl Lightning had just been chained in her stall when Drabik reached the barn. She had been showered and rubbed down and given a new, clean hood. Her bit had been replaced with the sheath-like gag. She could smell the cream from the rubdown as she stood confined, her back to the stall door. She was glad that she had not been sold. She didn't understand what had happened at the track, but everybody seemed pleased.

Drabik ordered one of the stable boys to blind her and take her up to the 'tack' room. It was more like a small barn. Maddy had been there a week ago to be measured for her racing harness. It had a large storage area in the back, and a large room in the front, where several ponies could be dealt with at once. Like all of the pony facilities, it had ample equipage for disciplining recalcitrant ponygirls.

It was the dark haired, twenty year old stable boy, Evan, who retrieved Maddy from her stall. She was surprised to be taken out so quickly, but her spirits were high and she actually looked forward to a passionate session with a trainer. She was unsettled when the stable boy lowered the flaps on her hood to cover her eyes, and even more so when he attached a leash to her nose ring and was led her out of the barn.

It was late afternoon, and the sky was darkening with an impending storm. Drabik waited outside of the 'tack' room. When he saw Lightning, he felt shamed at how readily he agreed to torment her for no reason other than to amuse the devilish daughter of his employer.

Maddy was nervous when she felt the floorboards of the tack room under her feet. The stable boy hitched her leash to a post and awaited instructions. Anya arrived a moment later and she was accompanied by another stable boy, the tall, blond one called Ivan.

"Anton, you've brought her. Good. And I've brought another big strapping lad to join in the fun."

"Let's get on with this," Drabik replied sullenly.

"I agree. But let me take a good look at her first. You've never even let me touch her."

Maddy was startled to hear the dark haired woman's voice. And was that her trainer's voice? She started to get nervous.

Anya walked up to the disconcerted pony and released her ring from the leash. "What lovely breasts," Anya said as she grabbed them with her hands. She caressed them softly. "So smooth and firm. Will you whip them for me, Anton?" she asked him playfully.

"Sure, Anya, whatever you want. Evan, get out the mounting cart," Drabik ordered.

Anya looked at where Maddy's face should have been. "Oh, you've got her eyes all closed up, Anton. I want her to see everything. It's no fun if she can't see." She lifted the flaps on Maddy's hood and exposed her tiny eyeholes. "Imagine that all you could see was from these tiny holes, Anton. How terrible it must be. But I think that she's recognized you."

Maddy had indeed recognized her former trainer. She was momentarily puzzled and then she realized that she was going to be put on show for the woman. As Anya slipped behind her, she emitted a little whine of unhappiness. Anya took her breasts from behind and squeezed them, presenting them to Drabik.

"Let's see if I can get her hot, Anton," the woman said. She rubbed Maddy's nipples with her palms, teasing them into hardness. If Drabik could have seen Maddy's face, he would have seen the look of utter dismay there and the piteous appeal for deliverance. But he could not see her face. All he could see was an inscrutable mask of blue. Maddy began to struggle in Anya's grasp. She could feel Anya's breasts pressing up against her back, her pelvis against her rear. Anya grabbed her nipples firmly. "She's skittish, Anton. Slap her across the breasts for me. She has to settle down if we're going to have any fun."

Drabik wavered momentarily. Then he came to his senses. "This is not a woman," he thought. "This is a pony. And she needs to be treated like a pony." He suddenly was filled with rage at the animal that he had trained. It reflected poorly on him.

The ponygirl trainer stepped forward. For a moment, Maddy thought that he was going to free her from the woman's grasp. But then she felt the woman release her breasts and hold her upper arms tightly, bending her back slightly so that her breasts were presented to the angry man in front of her. Drabik could not read Maddy's face, but she could read his.

He reared his right hand back and slapped Maddy viciously across her breasts. The blow stunned her and her breasts stung from the impact of his hand. He repeated the blow with his left, marking Maddy's right breast with the imprint of his hand. Maddy cried out in pain and sorrow. "How can he treat me this way?" she thought in despair.

Drabik repeated his blows across Maddy's large white mounds. Her knees weakened as her spirit faded. "Oh, God," she prayed, "please, not this!"

Anya's hands returned to Maddy's breasts, pinching the nipples fiercely. Her dark passions were stoked by the beating of the ponygirl. "Get her to her knees, Anton. I want to see her suck a cock," she said, her lust evident in her voice.

Maddy's former trainer snapped his fingers at his waist. Maddy, in hopeless misery, fell to her knees. Anya began to unfasten her gag. "Evan," she shouted, "come fuck this pony's mouth for us!"

Evan was more than willing. It would be exciting to have the lady from the big house see his prick in action. And Maddy's reputation for her oral skills was very high.

Maddy moaned as she saw Evan undoing his fly. She could not understand the words, but she was aware of the cruel tone of Anya's voice. And she saw the anger and determination in her master's face. In spite of all, she would do anything for him. She hated herself for needing him, for wanting him. "If this pleases him," she thought, "I'll do what he wants, I'll give the woman a good show."

Maddy opened her mouth meekly as Evan pressed his cock to her lips. Anya gave a squeal of delight and took a chair so that she could watch the pony's mouth at work in comfort.

Maddy obediently washed the dark haired boy's meat with her lips. She teased the head of his cock with her tongue, drawing a deep sigh from him. His hands rested lightly on her head as she drew her lips up and down his sturdy pole. She could sense the woman watching. And her master.

"Look how well she does it, Anton. Was this part of your training?" Anya asked him.

"Yes," he replied. "And I could train you too, if you like."

"Oh Anton," she said, laughing, "don't make promises that you can't keep."

Although Anya was willing to risk her father's approbation for her scandalous activities, she didn't want any rumors getting back to him about her nocturnal activities with his assassin.

But Grobgy already knew. He was no fool. Anya was watched like a hawk. He knew where she was right now. For some reason, he had looked the other way as far as Anton was concerned. "Maybe he's the one," he would think as he watched them together. He needed someone as hard and cruel as he for a son-in-law.

The stable boy groaned as Maddy took his cock down her throat. She had heard the whimsical banter between her trainer and the lady and could not help but feel shamed that she was performing this act in front of her, and that her trainer and master was watching her do it. For a moment, she thought she would collapse from despair.

She continued her oral manipulation of the stable boy's manhood. His tool was hot and rigid and he swayed as the pleasure of the pony's mouth flowed through him. Maddy could feel her naked breasts quivering as she moved her head back and forth to build the stable boy's need. In spite of her humiliation, Maddy's sex had begun to register a building passion of her own. Her cunt now responded automatically in an almost Pavlovian reaction when she came into contact with a hard prick. Her whole life was sex and running. And the whip. She hoped to avoid it tonight.

Anya got up from her chair. She was enthralled by the sight of Maddy's hungry lips on the boy's rod. She squatted down next to the pony and began to caress her breasts. "She's hot, Anton," she told her lover. "I bet I could make her come."

Drabik watched in silence as Anya continued to massage the pony's swollen breasts. Maddy moaned, unable to hold back her lust. "See!" Anya squealed with delight. "No wonder you like her so much!"

Anya's mocking tone was having its effect on Drabik. Anya was angry that he had spent so many nights fucking this stupid pony rather than her. She wanted to destroy any feelings Drabik had for her. She new of no better way than to anger Drabik into treating her as what she was, nothing more than a trained beast.

The stable boy's hips started to shake as he neared his climax. Maddy moaned as the delicate hands of the woman teased and stroked her nipples. There was no other sound in the room except for the pleasure induced sighs of the stable boy and the excited moans of the ponygirl. The stable boy began to grunt and thrust his hips at Maddy's mouth. Maddy gave a small whine as she felt her unwanted lusts building. Anya's hand descended between the pony's widespread thighs and slid her fingers between her distended lower lips.

"Oh! Oh! Oh!" the stable boy cried as he shot his load into Maddy's mouth. Maddy's orgasmic cries were stifled by the pulsing prick that filled her. "Oh, Anton, she's coming!" Anya laughed at her success. "She's coming all over my hand!"

Maddy cursed herself with each jolting contraction of her lush, blood filled pussy. Anya's fingers relentlessly teased her rigid clit. "Mhhhhhhhhh! Mhhhhhhh!" she moaned.

The boy was finished and he self consciously put his tool away. Anya still held Maddy's cunt in thrall. She turned to Drabik. "Let's have the blond boy fuck her while she's still hot!" she said excitedly.

Drabik nodded and the blond boy jumped to take his turn. The mounting cart was a wheeled framework used for whipping or fucking a pony. She could be held in various positions on it, exposing the desired portion of her body to caresses of blows. The blond boy, Ivan, grabbed Maddy away from Anya and pushed her face down over it. Broad straps went around her fixing her in place. The front end was cranked up so that Maddy's head was slightly higher than her rear. He legs were fixed wide apart. He rushed to unbutton his trousers. "I'll make her squeal,' he thought. Anya had picked up Maddy's gag and brought it over to where she was displayed.

"I think you need your gag, little pony," she said, tauntingly. Maddy opened her mouth obediently as the woman pushed it in. Maddy felt the nineteen year old boy behind her pushing his cock up against her loins. She whined in shame. Anya's face was not more than six inches away from hers. The gang leader's daughter was pleased. This was better than she had imagined it would be when she had started planning it weeks ago. Her hatred of the ponygirl who had stolen her lover's cock from her had festered for a while.

Anya heard Maddy sigh as the blond boy entered her. She looked up at him. "Not the pussy, boy, her ass. Fuck her ass!"

Ivan grinned and withdrew his solid pole from Maddy's sex. He pressed it at the entrance to her bowels. Maddy knew precisely what the effect the boy's prick would have as it scoured the tender tissue of her anal ring. She shook futilely in an attempt to free her self from the wooden frame. "Look, she likes it!" Anya exclaimed.

Maddy could not see her trainer through the dime sized holes in her hood. Her collar was held in place on the frame and she could not turn her head. But she sensed his presence and silently called out to him for help.

Drabik could only hear her frantic whines and see her blue clad shaking head. His heart had grown cold for the pony he had broken in and trained. She deserved this, he thought. They all did.

Maddy felt the stiff rod pass the entrance of her rear and fill her bowel. As it rasped across the delicate tissue surrounding it, her already moist and hot pussy began to react. She looked and saw the distorted, cruel face of the woman staring back at her. At that moment she realized that the woman hated her. She realized then that she was her trainer's mistress! The knowledge struck her like a blow from a fist. Maddy knew that she could expect no kindness or mercy from her.

Ivan was pumping furiously between Maddy's rear cheeks. Anya, with her face still looming in front of the pony's, reached under her chest and started to caress her dangling breasts. She pulled and teased the stiff nipples. The pony's head began to swirl as her lust was driven higher and higher. Although she tried, she could no longer stifle her passion. 'Ohhhhhhh!" she moaned from behind her gag. And, "Oh! Oh! Oh!" as she came. When she felt the blond stable boy's cock begin to pulse and jet his hot come inside her, she came again, moaning loudly, biting down on her gag in shame and self pity.

Anya stood, beaming with satisfaction. "You train your ponies well, Anton. She's a lustful beast. Now I want her tits whipped as you promised."

Maddy's body was turned around on the frame so that she was lying on her back, her legs splayed wide open, her head leaning backwards, suspended over the end. Her back was arched, raising her breasts to the whip. Drabik chose a four foot long, leather encased reed. Maddy heard it whoosh through the air as he tested it and realized that she was to be beaten. She squirmed her torso and flexed her distended legs in fear. Her sex lay exposed, her moist sheath glistening between her engorged labia.

Drabik stood in front of the cart and Maddy could see his legs and waist. She saw the whip in his hard, strong, right hand. She could not see his face or the grimace of disdain and anger drawn across it. Anya could see it and she knew that she had done her job well.

"Strike her hard, Anton," she said excitedly. "I want to see her body jump with each blow!"

The pony trainer lifted the whip above his head and brought it down hard on Maddy's exposed right breast. Her breast recoiled at the blow which landed astride her nipple. She arched her back in agony and moaned deeply, piteously through her gag. "Why is he doing this?" she thought in anguish. "Why?" Drabik landed a matching blow to Maddy's left orb producing another wave of searing pain. Maddy was terrified that he was going to rip her apart. She had seen his face lined with cruelty earlier and she knew that she could expect to mercy. Her bladder released its contents and her pussy emitted a yellow stream.

"She's pissed herself," cried Anya, delighted at the show so far. "Hit her again!"

Drabik drifted to his right and prepared to land another blow. He brought the reed down carefully across both of Maddy's tender mounds and she shrieked in agony. He centered himself between her legs and struck again, landing a blow on first her right breast and then her left in quick succession. Maddy's body jerked and spasmed in her bindings. The smell of her discharged urine filled the air. Her tortured moans filled the room.

Her tormentor needed no further encouragement from his mistress. He circled round the poor pony three times, striking out at her now bright red breasts every few seconds. When he came to a stop at the front of the frame, he took in the vision of the crying, moaning pony. He saw her splayed legs and the tempting target between her thighs. His blood lust was on him and he yearned to crush all of the feelings for this female that he had felt poisoning him, diluting his power. He stood with the pony's head between his legs and raised the cane high.

Maddy intuitively realized his target and began to shake and convulse, pulling desperately on the bonds that held her ankles at almost right angles to her body. She screamed unformed words of entreaty to her master that emerged from her gag as a cacophony of high pitched whines. When Drabik struck, expertly driving the last four inches of the shaft between Maddy's hairless, tender labial lips, the pony wrenched and twisted in pain. Her whole body shuddered and quaked. Her voice was hoarse with her screams, and a low growl of pain radiated from her throat. Three times the enraged ponygirl trainer and assassin placed his well aimed blows on Maddy's cunt. Her world was a torrent of agony. The poor girl yearned for death, miserable that her master should subject her to such wicked torments.

And then it was over. The only sound in the room was Maddy's woeful moans as the pain continued to flow through her from her damaged slit and breasts. They throbbed with continuous burning pain. But Drabik was not finished dealing with his former charge. He needed one last act of domination to satisfy his wrath. He spun Maddy's cart so that he could avoid the small pool of urine that had formed below her. He took a rough cloth and wiped away the traces of her discharge from her loins. And then he loosened his fly, freeing his rampant cock.

Anya's blood was on the boil. She was enraptured with her triumph over the lowly ponygirl. And when she saw Drabik draw his sword of flesh, she shouted out to encourage him, "Do it, Anton, fuck her worthless cunt!"

Drabik stepped between the crying and moaning pony's legs. He could see her owner's crest stretched out on her taut belly. He felt like that rampant wolf, preparing to consume its victim. He insinuated his hard cock between Maddy's burning nether lips. She had been lost in another dimension, where she could separate her mind from her tortured flesh. The pressure of Drabik's hot meat between her legs brought her back. She knew whose cock that was. As she felt it slide within her, she reexperienced the wave of revulsion she felt when he had first penetrated her many weeks ago. She moaned in despair that she should have to bear such infamies. Her body yearned to expel the invader and her knees and hips shook in a frantic and hopeless attempt to do so. She felt the hot meat push open her sheath, filling her cavity.

The man reveled in his victory over the now despised ponygirl. Her cunt wrapped tightly around his cruel prick sending a wave of pleasure through him. He was determined to make her come, to prove his mastery over her. He fucked her in long, slow thrusts, dragging his cock against her stiff pleasure bud. Anya had crept to the front of the cart and had put out her hands to seized Maddy's tortured breasts. Drabik looked up at her and snarled, "Don't touch her!"

Anya recoiled in fear. She had known of Drabik's reputation for hardness and cruelty, but she had never seen him like this. She resolved never to be the subject of his wrath.

Maddy's eyes were jammed shut, in shame and sorrow. She felt her lusts begin to rise as her hole was relentlessly plowed. She had given up her doomed efforts to expel Drabik's hated member from her sheath. She knew that she could not fight him, that he would win. The need for completion overrode the pain of her brutalized slit. She let the wave of her rising lust flow through her. Her need carried her away. She cried out as the male member drove her closer and closer to the unwanted orgasm. She made one last, futile effort to forestall Drabik's victory over her. She bit down on her gag, tensed her muscles, even clamped the muscles of her hot crevasse down around the meat that pierced her. If only she could still the relentless friction on her hardened pleasure bud, she could hold out, resist the irresistible. But the waters of her lust broke through the dam of her resistance. Her thighs began to quiver and her heart began to pound in her chest. Her breasts were hard and sore with her need. "Ohhhhhhhhhhhhh!!" she moaned as her passion crested. "Ohhhhhhhhhhhh!"

Her mind was cleared of all thoughts other than the absorption of the waves of pleasure that the hard spasms of her pussy sent there. They washed away all resistance and she let her body float in a sea of ecstasy.

Drabik felt Maddy's cunt throb and contract around his prick. He had won his victory over the ponygirl. With a roar he let his own passions flow, jetting his hot sperm inside her. His hips pounded hers as he felt all of his anger and resentment against her released and poured into her helpless body through his loins. The ponygirl would fear him once more. She would quail as he dragged her from her stall to torment her. She would quiver when she was sent to her knees to receive his lust. And she would know that her will was bent to his, that her body belonged not to her, but to her betters, her masters.

When Maddy felt her trainer's cock release its hot load into her belly, her mind clouded anew with passion. She hated herself as her cunt convulsed, abjuring the pleasure even as it electrified her body and mind. Yes, she belonged to her master. His will was hers. She was nothing, he was all.

CHAPTER SIX

It was several weeks after his meeting with Sergi that Jake received in the mail a round trip ticket to Dlitski. Mary Ellen had supervised the delivery of two shipments to Khalid, eighteen girls in all, and payments had been received in due course. There was a set scale based on the finer details of the slave's anatomy and appearance. Pictures were taken of them showing all of their assets and flaws and sent on to Khalid in Kalikastan. He would post offers based on the ratings. There was some give or take about the girl's qualifications and a price was agreed upon. Mary Ellen was a shrewd bargainer and he let her deal with the coded emails that flew between each end of this segment of the distribution chain.

There were several other buyers who would email requests. Jake was more reticent about replying to them for fear that they might be part of some sting. Those emails were answered by "all future negotiations must be done in person until further notice." Once the real identities of the buyers were determined, and their bona fides checked out, business would resume as usual.

Mary Ellen had also proved adept at the acquisition end. Chuckie had accompanied her on four or five trips to independents around the east from Little Rock to Boston, from Detroit to Tuscaloosa. After two weeks, at which point she had established her own bona fides, she and her girlfriend Vicki dropped Chuckie in a hole somewhere in Ohio. End of problem.

Jake boarded the Aeroflot jet with some trepidation. He couldn't carry any hardware on the plane and he assumed that he would be picked up at the airport. He had made contact with some underworld elements in Dlitski but he wasn't sure how he was going to meet up with them. And he wasn't sure that he wouldn't be dropped in a hole somewhere on the Kalikastan steppes either. But business was going well and that was usually insurance against problems.

He had in his briefcase a written proposal for a bottle factory to be located in the Kalikastan heartland, near the Bremski River. But it was merely cover. Once he had ascertained the level of interest in forming an alliance with his principal, the real negotiations would begin between Khalid's boss and his.

The flight was uneventful and after he cleared customs, such as it was, he walked out of the terminal, his overnight and valise in his hands. A short, scrappy looking driver was sitting outside of a black Mercedes. He nodded at Jake and Jake got in. In forty five minutes, they pulled into Khalid's compound.

Khalid was there to greet him, Sergi by his side. The fat man was effusive and gregarious.

"Mr. Wilson, if that's the name you like, welcome to Kalikastan. Please accept my hospitality," Khalid said, grinning ear to ear. Jake assumed that Mr. Burnham had checked out okay.

He and Burnham had sat down weeks before and laid out the plan. Burnham had enough business clout to deliver millions of dollars to Kalikastan in contracts and investments. He also had a lead on the construction of the proposed gas and petroleum pipelines that were to run through Kalikastan to the West. The line would save a hundred million dollars in reduced construction costs by avoiding the necessity to cross the Urals. During the contemplated two years of construction it would be Wild West City and whoever knew the route would be able to set up their 'pleasure' operations to take advantage of the pocket money of the thousands of workers.

Burnham had juice and Khalid's people were very interested. Jake's trip was for the purpose of setting up a meeting between principals. But his real task was to begin tracing the whereabouts of Madeline. Burnham would continue to dangle the bait while he went on the prowl.

"Your latest shipment arrived earlier today," Khalid told him, waving his arm at a line of naked, collared and bound females standing in a line side by side on the cobblestone courtyard. Although they wore shield like gags across their lower faces, he recognized them from the pictures that had been sent last week. Jake made it a practice not to go down into the basement of the uniform rental warehouse except when necessary. True to her word, Mary Ellen had a couple of her 'girls' minding the inmates, along with Allison, Feeney's left over prisoner. He didn't want to see them, know them or anything else. A job was a job and anything that was necessary to complete the job would be done. That was his code and his reputation. This case, although the scale of wrongdoing dwarfed anything he had done before, was no exception.

The young girls' eyes darted nervously about them as they stood, naked, awaiting the next development in their nightmare. Khalid had set up a post in the courtyard about fifteen feet in front of them. A small blond haired girl was dangling from it, her hands up above her chained to a gibbet that extended from its top. She probably stood about 5'3". To Jake, she had looked to be about 20 or 21 years old

"I was just about to entertain these pretty girls with a demonstration of my talents with a whip. Would you like to watch?"

Jake would like nothing less, but he was playing the role, in his own words, of a cold and barbarous slaver. What difference would a little whipping mean to him?

"Lovely," Jake replied. He had to admit that he had wondered what it would be like and the thought of all that unused female flesh sitting in the basement of his uniform company had been starting to get at him. He watched as an obsequious servant handed Khalid a long, black whip. Khalid cracked it into the air twice, drawing moans from the assembled young women. The girl on the gibbet was frantic. Her eyes were as wide as saucers. Jake could see the sweat produced by her nervous apprehension glistening on her body.

One of Khalid's henchmen removed the girl's gag. She started to plead with the heartless slaver. "Please mister, please don't whip me! I'll do anything that you say! Please!"

The girl had beautiful round breasts that swayed as she begged for mercy. But mercy was in short supply at Khalid's. He swung his whip back and landed a blow atop the girl's right breast. A big red mark appeared immediately, and the girl's screams punctuated the courtyard. "Ahhhhhhh!" she yelled as she danced in her chains. A second blow landed, expertly thrown, atop her left breast. The girl repeated her piteous wail. Now she was screaming her supplications. "Oh, God, please don't do this, please! I'll do anything, please! Oh, no!"

The last was uttered as Khalid reared back for another blow from the whip. It cracked loudly as it struck her lower belly, just above her pubis. "Ahhhhhhh!" the girl screamed as a bright red blotch rose up on her stomach. Her legs collapsed underneath her.

Khalid, smiling, said to Jake, "Watch this." He swung the whip back and stepping closer to the girl hurled the whip end at her. It circled around her torso and struck her buttocks. She leapt in the air as the blow registered in her brain. "Ohhhhh!" she cried out, tears pouring down her face. Her eyes were red from crying, and her mouth was downturned in a dismal frown. As Khalid raised the whip one more time, she tried to shie away from him, stretching her arms to their limit, pulling the chain taut away from her tormentor. The greasy slavemaster threw the whip one last time and it cracked directly between the young woman's legs. "Ohhhhhhhhh! Nooooooo! Please stop, please!" she called out, mournfully frantic.

Khalid rested the whip at his side and the gag was restored to the moaning girl's mouth. She sagged in her chain, obviously relieved that her torment was over. In actuality, it had just begun. But her whipping was over, for today.

Turning to the cowering line of bound females, Khalid pointed the handle of the whip down the line and back up. He stopped it at the face of a shapely red headed girl. She was tall and thin and had small pointed breasts. Her well formed legs were long and there was an abundant reddish thatch between her thighs. Her arms were bound behind her. She whined as she saw Khalid select her. Khalid's man ran behind her and released her gag. She started to plead with the dark, flabby man, but he grabbed her cheeks and squeezed them tight. "No talking allowed, whore!" he boomed at her. She nodded, desperate not to trigger his wrath. He spoke to her politely. "Please get down on your knees and suck my cock, whore."

Obviously frantic the woman descended to her knees. A crowd of swarthy men had gathered around the young women. Sergi stood by Jake's side appraising his reactions. He still had his doubts about the American and his basket of goodies.

Khalid withdrew his fat prick from his pants and presented it to the young red head. Grimacing, she took it into her mouth and began to ministrate to it with her lips and tongue. Jake watched her work almost eagerly to please the fat man. This girl had been in his custody eighteen hours ago. Seventy two hours ago she was locked in some basement or closet, or in some underground pit, awaiting an unknown fate. Forty eight hours before that, more or less, she had been a free woman, for whom all was still possible. Her prospects for self fulfillment had diminished appreciably since then. He felt a tinge of sorrow for the girl. But then, he thought, what was she to him? He had a job to do and she was a sacrifice towards its completion.

Khalid's eyes rolled back as the girl continued to work on his tool. The other girls stared straight ahead, apparently afraid that if they watched the torment of their companion too closely, it would rub off on them. Suddenly Khalid let out a loud growl. He grabbed the head of the girl at his feet and pushed it down hard on his cock. She struggled as the fat prick descended down her throat. Khalid held her head there for a good minute as he waited for his cock to wind down its ejaculations. When he was satisfied he was done, he pulled his meat from her lips.

At a signal, his men stepped up to the other women and removed their gags. There were unceremoniously pushed to their knees. The men lined up before them, two or three to a girl and awaited their turn for oral copulation. The young women whined and cried as their mouths were pried open, but they all quickly fell to their tasks without strenuous objection.

Tucking his cock back into its home, Khalid smiled at Jake. "You send me good cunt, Mr. Wilson. I'm very grateful. Tomorrow I'm due a load of Spaniards. Very hot!"

"I'm sure, Mr. Khalid," Jake said. "But if you show me to my room, I'd like to take a shower and freshen up a bit. It was a long flight."

"Certainly, Mr. Wilson. Here," he said, pointing to the blond girl who had just been whipped, "take her with you with my complements. I'm sure she'll do anything you ask." He laughed heartily.

Khalid's servant handed Jake a leash with the blond girl's collar connected to it. "Achmed will show you to your room. Have fun!" Khalid told him. Jake heard Khalid issue an order to the factotum in the local Slavic dialect. Achmed led Jake up a set of stairs and halfway around the courtyard. A door led to a hallway with a series of doors. Achmed opened one and admitted Jake and his companion. He put Jake's bags down on the floor, nodded with a lugubrious smile on his face and left.

The bedroom consisted of a large king sized bed, a table with some straight backed chairs and a cabinet on the far wall. The room had a luxurious bathroom with a sunken tub with an overhead shower. There was a large mirror along one wall of the bathroom and on the ceiling of the bedroom. There were rings on the head and footboards, presumably for tying off the hands and feet of slave girls.

Jake turned to the blond that he had towed along with him. She stood about shoulder height to him and he was only 5'7". Her hair was long and straight, wheat colored. She wore a fine tan and a tiny, alabaster white triangle on each breast, with light pink nipples. Her bush was bikini trimmed, with a little tuft above the pale white skin of her sex and narrow slivers of white going over her hips. The girl was crying silently, but steadily. The whip had made deep maroon bruises on her breasts and her lower belly.

Not knowing what else to do with the girl, he ordered her up on the bed. "Kneel there until I want you," he told her. He tied off her leash to a ring in the center of the headboard. He didn't think she would run, but you never knew. It wasn't the way he wanted to start things off, having a slave girl book on him.

The girl's body was bent over as she had to lower her head to accommodate the leash tied to the ring. Her hands were tied behind her and she wore a thick, leather collar. She had scrunched her legs under her and Jake could see the soles of her feet sitting under her tight, pert rear globes. He removed his clothes and stepped into the bathroom.

The heat of the shower water was soothing to him. After soaping and rinsing his hair and body, he stood there, mesmerized by it. He started thinking about the glorious body of the young, American, blond woman kneeling on his bed. Although she was slender and small, her breasts were round and full. He thought of how they quivered as she stood there crying in front of him. He imagined sucking on the pale nipples, cupping the half melon sized breasts with his hands. He loved her golden tanned body. He bet that she was a real beach girl, probably from Florida or the Gulf Coast. Maybe even New Jersey, although it was still a little early for a decent tan in the Northeast.

Jake's cock began to stiffen and he instinctively ran his hand down its rubbery length. It had been a while since he had gotten his dick wet, not since Chicago, at least a month ago. His mind recalled the tall coffee-colored whore, Jackie, and her skilled and playful mouth. His cock had grown rampant from his handling of it and he felt a little thrill as his hand ran across the tender skin surrounding its helmet. He was tempted to pull it to completion, but that would be foolish with a pretty, servile, young lass kneeling on his bed awaiting his instructions. She had said that she would do anything. And it wasn't as if she wasn't going to be raped twenty or thirty times before the week was out, and by men much less kindly than him.

He turned off the water and stepped out of the shower. He ran the heavy, thick and plush bath towel over his body and hair. When he was dry, he stepped back into the bedroom. The girl was still kneeling hunchbacked on the bed where he had left her. She must not have heard him come in because when he grabbed his pack of Luckies from the dresser where he had tossed it, and lit one up, she gave a little jump of surprise. He took a deep drag off of the softly packed cigarette and let out a plume of blue gray smoke. It drifted across the room and beclouded the form of the kneeling young woman.

Jake decided that he needed a drink. He opened the cabinet on the wall and, in addition to numerous selections of alcoholic beverages, there was mounted on the inside of the doors a variety of instruments of torment. There were whips, of course, but also nipple clamps, long, narrow needles, leather handcuffs, a ring gag and a small Taser like gun which plugged into the wall and had several long leads with clamps on the end. He looked back at the obedient young girl whose sniffles he could still discern. These were all in her future, he realized. She had been reduced to a commodity, an instrument of pleasure. And if some people's idea of pleasure was causing a defenseless young woman physical agony, then she would suffer it.

He grabbed a bottle of gin and poured himself three fingers. He sat in a leather padded chair across from the foot of the bed. The girl's fine ass confronted him and he could see the very tail end of her slit peaking out at the bottom of its graceful curves. His cock had grown hard again, and he sat in the chair naked, one hand holding three ounces of tart, nutmeg flavored gin and the other almost absent mindedly caressing his stiff rod.

"There are probably bugs in this room," he thought to himself. "Maybe even a camera." How would it look if the hard core slaver that he pretended to be neglected to tear off a piece of the pretty pussy sitting on his bed and only awaiting his command to spread her legs or open her mouth? That was, if not the deciding factor, at least the one he would use to justify what he did next.

Jake shot back most of the booze in his glass. The sharp tasting, transparent liquor burned as it went down. He put the glass aside, put out his cigarette and stood up. The girl must have heard him stir because she emitted a low moan. A moan of fear. Jake climbed on the bed and positioned himself behind the girl. He loosened the leash from her collar, reaching around her body with his hands. Doing so, his chest pressed against her back and her bound hands. His stiff cock nestled in the valley between her pale white, rear cheeks. The girl gave a little whine as she felt his body's heat against hers. What she had prayed and feared would not happen, but certainly knew would, was beginning.

Wordlessly, Jake pulled on the girl's tanned shoulders and had her raise her torso so that she was sitting on her haunches. He ran his hands over her soft, firm breasts, breathing in the aroma of her long, blond hair. When kneeling, her head came up just under his chin. His widespread thighs encompassed hers as he knelt behind her, drawing her in to his zone of control. He worried the girl's dainty nipples until they became stiff. As he caressed her breasts, massaging them slowly and gently with his hands, the girl gave a great sigh. It was a sigh of despair and of developing passion.

Jake's cock ached with need, but he was determined to wait until the girl had reached a peak of sexual excitement before entering her. While continuing to massage her breasts with one hand, he ran his other over her taut belly and down over her thighs. She had her knees pressed closely together as if she could bar his way to her private place. Jake ran his hands over her slender hips, up along her sides and under her breasts. Grabbing them lightly, but securely, he pushed them upwards, causing the girl to raise to her height, He grabbed the stiff nipples and pulled on them, extending her breasts, and then pinching them firmly, just enough to send an electrified sensation of discomfort to the girl's mind. The girl moaned with pleasure. In spite of herself, she was succumbing to Jake's campaign. He dropped his hands and pressed them inside of her tightly joined thighs and began to pull them apart. The girl resisted slightly, but then gave in to the strong pressure of Jake's hands.

Placing one arm around the girl's torso, holding her body closely pinned to his, Jake searched for the girl's tender slit with the other. His long fingers found it, and began to rub gently at the little nub at the apex, causing the girl to cry and moan at the same time. He felt her body loosen, as it gave in to the pleasurable waves that flowed through it. As he probed her moist sheath, the girl unconsciously spread her legs wider to ease his access. Jake held her neck in thrall with his vice-like left hand, arching her body back, while his right one plundered her steaming crevasse.

The girl's breaths were growing deeper and deeper. She was no longer crying, but had given in to the physical pleasure that Jake had imposed on her. When she moaned and began to gently thrust her hips at his hand, Jake pushed her torso forward, bending her back, until her forehead was in contact with the bed. He reached his hands under her from behind and raised her back side until her widespread and engorged lips were poised to receive him. He slowly and gently probed the opening with his cock. The girl, realizing in spite of her passion that the moment that she had feared had come, uttered a low, soulful, "Noooooo!" Her irresolute protest was cut off when Jake glided his hot tube of meat deep into her welcoming canal.

Jake luxuriated in the tight heat of her passage. His balls were tight and sore. Slowly, deliberately, he stroked his cock inside her, reigniting her feeble entreaties. "Oh, please, no, please, please," she murmured as her hips sought to match Jake's rhythm. "Oh,…oh,…oh,…please, oh, no, please don't, please," she moaned as her heat built. Jake felt himself ready to explode. He was holding his orgasm back until the girl had reached her crisis. Suddenly, "Oh!" she exclaimed loudly, and her hips began to rock and her hot tunnel clamp down hard on Jake's prick. "Ohhhhhhhhhhh!" she cried out as she came, her hands behind her clenched tightly together, her head buried between her knees.

The two lustful beings slammed against each other as their bodies convulsed with pulses of exquisite pleasure. Jake could feel his balls empty as he shot his load inside the slave girl's womb. He groaned as he felt his cock give its last throb. He was leaning on the girl's back. His hands had grabbed her shoulders when he began to come and he softened his grip. He could feel the girl's contractions on his cock as they began to fade. Jake ran his hands over her back and the outside of her thighs, consuming the tactile sensation of her soft flesh. He pulled back and his flaccid meat slid out of the girl's sex, slimy with their commingled juices.

The girl was crying again. Jake slapped her sharply on her buttocks. "Turn around," he ordered. Slowly, the girl rotated her body on the bed. Her eyes were red and tears flowed down her cheeks. Jake grabbed her hair behind her head and pushed her head down. He was annoyed at her bawling, and probably driven by guilt for his rape of the beautiful, innocent girl.

"Clean off my cock!" he ordered her in a stern, demanding voice. The girl obediently sucked in his tool and drove her lips down its length. The moist warmth of her mouth thrilled him and sent a shiver of pleasure through him. His prick began to stiffen right away. He had intended only to remove the girl's viscous discharge from his meat, but the heat of her mouth and the tightness of her lips had reignited his lust.

The girl whined as his cock hardened in her mouth. He began to rock his hips at her, running his cock over her lips and tongue. He had hold of her hair and used his grip to force her head into the desired rhythm. He felt a sudden rush at the freedom that he had to use this girl's body without regard for her feelings or pleasure. The girl gasped and coughed as he jammed his cock against the entrance of her throat. As he withdrew, he felt her tongue slide along his shaft, her lips drag across its skin as the girl tried to accelerate his orgasm. He pumped into her mouth again and again as his lust rose. And then, as he gave a deep, throaty growl, his cock exploded again, shooting his creamy ejaculation into the girl's helpless mouth.

Jake bent over, letting his softening prick lie in the girl's mouth. He felt her urge her head forward as it shrank, doubtless fearful to release it. "So this is what it is like," he mused as he pushed the girl back and withdrew his limp dick from between her lips. "Now I understand."

He ordered the girl to stand in the corner while he dressed. When he had donned fresh clothes, he opened the cabinet and pulled out a leather gag, much like the ones the other girls had been wearing when he arrived. He called the girl over and presented it to her mouth. She grimaced and shrank from him.

"P,please, sir, may I use the bathroom," she asked in a tiny fearful voice. Jake nodded and led her into the luxurious, tiled room. He watched as she sat on the toilet and emptied her bladder. He made her lean over and spread her legs so that he could wipe her. His hand lingered on her bearded cunt. He squeezed the labial lips lightly. He wondered how many men would pierce these lips in the next year of this young girl's life. He had been the first to enter her without her consent. And he had loved every minute of it. "What does that make me?" he asked himself. Then he shook himself. Philosophy was for the philosophers, he thought. He was a man of action and had no time for doubts or indecision. He had assumed the role of a slaver and he would do what a slaver would do.

Jake ordered the young girl to stand up and he pushed the gag into her mouth and locked it behind her head. A pair of pretty, anxious eyes peered above the leather shield that hid the lower portion of her face. Jake retrieved the leash from the ring on the bed and hooked it to the naked young girl's collar. He opened the door and led her into the hallway and then out onto the veranda that ran around the courtyard. Achmed was waiting there for him, smiling his lecherous smile. Jake handed the girl's leash to him and watched him lead the naked slave girl down the stairs. The girl looked up at him with her frightened eyes. "I never even asked her her name," Jake thought.

* * * * * * * * * * * * *

After concluding his mistreatment of the ponygirl he had named Lightning, Drabik and Anya had left the tack room. Anya was in a hurry to get Drabik into a bed and harvest the remnants of his passion. Ivan and Evan were in no hurry to leave and took their turns plowing Maddy's available, soggy sex. They left her there in the fading light.

Maddy spent the evening lying on her back, her legs spread in the lonely darkness. Although she had often spent long nights in darkness in the barn, at least there she could hear the sounds of the other ponies shifting about or the watchman on his rounds. Here there was just dead silence and it gave her much time for thought.

She was sure that her trainer's abuse of her had just begun in earnest. She had detected a look of hatred in his eyes, although she could not fathom what she had done to earn it. She shivered as she considered it. Cold, impersonal lust was one thing, but fierce, hot, malevolent anger was another. She was sure that she could expect a steady stream of painful and humiliating abuse from him. That devil woman had unleashed some demon in him. And from her exuberant enjoyment of her torment, Maddy knew that she could expect one day to be at that shewolf's mercy.

Her sex was sore where it had been struck and she could feel the swollen tissues throb during the long night.

Her breasts, too were swollen and her nipples felt ready to burst off of her body.

Although scenes from her former life still sprung into her mind from time to time, this night she felt more distant from it than ever before. Everything that came before she had been made into a ponygirl seemed like a pasteboard mockery of reality, done in black and white. The present was real and full of color, the color of welts and blood, the bright yellow of her owner's tattoo on her belly, the sinister dark blue of the hoods or the, for her, meaningless Cyrillic writing etched onto her chest. When not in darkness, she lived in the pale blue of the almost cloudless sky, the deep greens of the grass and the trees around her. There was no other reality, no loss to mourn for, since she could not believe anything else ever really existed.

But there was hope. Yesterday, she had felt threatened by the man in the beret. She was afraid that he had come to take her away and that she would never see her master again. But her trainer had destroyed whatever love she had for him, a love drawn from her desperate need to hold on to some humanity, even if it was for a man who had stripped her of the rest. Tonight, as she patiently waited for sleep to claim her, Maddy hoped that his seeming approval of her and her harness mate, the pony she knew only as the blond tailed pony with large saucer like areola and thick, red nipples, meant that he would claim them.

Maddy's stomach growled as it yearned for food, yet she had no desire for it, the tasteless mash that she had supped on for many weeks. She was sure that it was full of vitamins and nutrients necessary for the strenuous life of a ponygirl. And she was sure that it contained something that barred any chance of pregnancy from the steady stream of sperm poured into her defenseless crevasse. Her period had not come either, and she suspected that her masters controlled that as well.

Lying on her back, her legs spread as if in invitation to the ghosts that surely haunted the grounds of this hell on earth, Maddy finally felt the mercy of sleep descend over her. She prayed for a dreamless night.

* * * * * * * * * * * * *

In a third story room over a tavern about thirty miles from Grobgy's estate, the black haired pirate's daughter too had her legs splayed wide. She was receiving the thrusts of her dark, fearsome lover. The room was lit by the dim glow of a small lamp sitting on a table by the window. The room was furnished in the style of a rich peasant, with a large, soft, bed, with tall posts on each corner. The furniture was heavy and made of dark wood. The walls were adorned with colorful, flowered wallpaper. In the middle of the room was a large, circular rug made of thick wool. The dark red rug was strewn with the lovers' clothes, as if they had shed them hurriedly in their drive for the stage where their passion would be played out. The windows had white, lacy chintz curtains and hanging on the walls were portraits of the Czars, taken from some secret storage place after the downfall of the Soviet State.

Anya was thrusting madly as Drabik's cock plunged mercilessly inside her. She was on the edge of bliss and her body yearned desperately to tumble over it. Drabik roared as his cock began to shoot its juice into Anya's steaming hole. When she felt his cock throbbing within her, she came, shouting his name. Drabik held her hands tightly together over her head and had forced his demanding tongue into her mouth. She felt doubly invaded as wave after wave of lust filled spasms jolted her.

As their passions faded, Drabik collapsed on Anya's wilted body. Their chests heaved together, Anya's pale white bosoms crushed flat against her. It was several minutes before they spoke. "Anton, darling, let me up, I have to pee," Anya panted.

Drabik rolled off of her and to his back. "Oh, God in heaven," he swore, "you have a marvelous cunt, Anya, and I know cunts."

Anya laughed as she crawled off of the bed. "I might say the same thing about your cock, Anton, but I guess I haven't had nearly as many cocks as you have had cunts."

She padded into the small bathroom and peed with the door open. Drabik's eyes were on the ceiling, however as he pondered the day's events. He had felt satisfied that he had broken the spell that the ponygirl had placed on him. But had he? Although he had beaten her unmercifully and driven her to orgasm on his own terms, he still felt a lingering connection to his former charge. What had made him so angry, he asked himself. Was it the fact that he had felt something for the abject beast? Was it because she was to be taken away from him, albeit for only six short weeks while she traveled the ponygirl circuit? Or was it because Anya had taunted him, unmanned him, having detected his bond with the female?

"Get the vodka," he called to Anya as she stood from her seat.

The tall, slim, white skinned beauty grabbed the bottle from the floor where it had been dropped when they came in the room. There were glasses on the table and she brought them too. She cracked open the seal and poured two large shots. She jumped into the bed and handed one over to her lover. They both poured them directly into their throats.

"Give me another," Drabik snarled.

"What makes you so ornery?" she asked him as she complied with his order.

"I'm always ornery when I fuck a beautiful, black haired bitch," he retorted.

Anya laughed. "You're right to call me a bitch, Anton, and you'd better call me beautiful." Drabik grunted in reply.

"Another," Drabik ordered. Anya filled his glass and her own. The fiery liquid was consumed in one gulp.

Anya put her glass down and snuggled up to the scar ridden body of the cruel ponygirl trainer. She reached over and grabbed his long, thick, limp cock. Cum still leaked from its tip and she leaned over and licked it off with her tongue. She smiled at Drabik, her hand still fondling his piece. "How many bullets do you have left in your pistol, Anton? You gave one away to that slut of a ponygirl. That belonged to me."

Drabik lifted his head and glared at the gangster's daughter. He reached out and grabbed her by the cheeks, pushing them together until Anya grimaced and squealed. "Nothing is yours unless I give it to you, slut," Drabik told her, his voice ominous.

As he let go, Anya tried to sidestep Drabik's hostility. "I love it when you call me names," she answered him. His cock was growing to hardness in her hand. "You were going to teach me to suck cock like a ponygirl, Antonushka," she said, laughing.

Drabik looked at the brazen young woman. "Why not?" he thought.

"First another drink, to get in the mood," he suggested. Anya poured two more shots. They threw them back. "Another!" he demanded.

"Okay, lover, but why drink so fast. I'm not used to this stuff," Anya answered. They drank again.

"And one more for good luck!" he cried.

Anya grinned at him. "Okay, okay, one more."

Drabik watched the black haired girl suck down the potent vodka. He put his glass down. "I'll be right back," he promised. He got up from the bed and went into the bathroom. While he was pissing, he looked around and saw the cords for the blinds on the windows. But how to cut them! There was a glass on the sink for drinking water. He picked it up and dropped it on the white porcelain. It smashed. "Fuck!" he yelled.

"What happened," Anya asked.

"I broke the fucking glass!" Drabik answered. "Give me a minute to clean it up." He peaked over his shoulder and saw that Anya was not looking. He took one of the larger shards and used it to cut the cords. He had two, four foot long cords. There was a bathrobe on the back of the door with a cotton sash. He removed it. Hiding his treasures behind his back, he returned to the bed. Anya was looking glassy eyed. He snuck the bindings under the pillow and rolled his body on to hers, covering her mouth with his. He thrust his tongue deep inside. Anya threw her arms around him and returned his passion. She locked her legs with his and pressed her loins against his thigh. "Mmmmmmmmmmmm!" she moaned as her blood began to rise.

Drabik ran his hand down her belly and buried it in her thick, black curly bush. He found her wet slit and caressed its length, pressing his fingers inside. He whispered in her ear, "So you want me to teach you how to suck cock like a ponygirl? Are you sure?"

"Ohhhh, yes," Anya sighed as she felt her loins get hot.

Sliding one hand under the pillow, he removed the cotton sash. He grabbed one of her wrists and while pressing his tongue back into her mouth, wrapped one end of the sash around it and tied it off.

"What are you doing, Antonushka?" the woman asked dreamily. The vodka she had downed so quickly, in combination with her lustful feelings, had made her lethargic.

"Roll over, sweetheart," he whispered to her, using his hands to lift her side and roll it over.

"Wha…." Anya started to ask, startled at Drabik's sudden movement. The experienced slaver quickly had both her wrists tied behind her.

"What are you doing, Anton?" she asked nervously. He rolled her over again onto her back.

"Ponygirls don't have hands, Anya," he said, grinning sardonically at her. He reached under the pillow and grabbed the other cords. He turned quickly and sat over Anya's thighs. He grabbed one ankle and tied a cord around it, and then the other.

Anya was beginning to get nervous. "Please Anton, stop," she intoned anxiously. "What are you doing to me?"

Without responding, Drabik tied one of Anya's ankles to one of the posts at the foot of the bed. While she stared at it in shock, he grabbed the other ankle and tied it off on the opposite post.

The black haired woman told him petulantly, "Anton, untie me! Have you lost your mind?" She sat up in emphasis. Drabik pushed her body back down and covered her with his own. He placed his mouth on one of her thick, stiff nipples and sucked on it long and hard. Anya moaned and squirmed underneath him.

"Anton!" she said with a little less force, "you've got to untie me, now!"

Drabik shifted to the other nipple and ran his hand between her outstretched thighs. Anya moaned again as he delved into her already dilated sex. When she tried to speak again, he brought his mouth to hers and kissed her. She kissed him back passionately, his hand driving her lust higher and higher. When he thought that he had her hot enough, he crept up the length of her body. His cock was hard and ready to garner her mouth's caresses. He spun around so that he was turned opposite from her and kneeling above her head. He ran his hands over her fine breasts, appreciating their bulk and their firmness. He pinched the nipples until the girl gave out a deep moan. "Oh, Anton," she sighed, "what are you doing?"

Drabik slid his hands up towards Anya's throat and then captured her head in them. He turned her head backwards so that she was looking up towards the headboard. Her face was upside down to his. He pushed his hips forward. "Open your mouth, little flower," he cooed to her. "Let my hot prick in."

He pushed his cock against her swollen lips and she opened them in obedience. She had sucked his cock before, but on her terms and always as preparation for a fuck. She had refused to let him come in her mouth, never mind swallow it. As his thick prick crossed her lips, Anya whined. "Ommmmpf!" she mumbled as the round bulk of Drabik's stiff rod suppressed her speech.

"Don't talk, Anya, suck. Suck my cock like the whore you are," he sad to her sternly. Anya desperately circled Drabik's meat with her lips. He luxuriated in her moist heat and the swirling of her tongue around its tip. He pulled back and forth gently, careful not to frighten his bound lover. He could see her splayed legs jerk and pull at her bindings, testing their strength. Her cunthole glistened with her lust.

As the man's member reveled in her mouth, Anya began to get worried. She had no way to stop him from coming in her mouth, no way to push him off of her. The anxious woman began to twist and turn her legs in an effort to free them. But Drabik knew his business and the knots were tied tight. She moaned and whined, hoping to convey her displeasure as the rock solid meat rasped against her lips.

"So, Anya, are you ready to learn to suck a cock like a ponygirl?" Drabik asked her tauntingly. Anya tried to speak, but her words were blocked by Drabik's prick. She tried to shake her head to free her mouth of the invasive tool, but Drabik held her head steady.

"Here it comes, Anya, get ready!"

Drabik pushed his manhood deep into Anya's oral cavity. She felt it depress her tongue and push up against the entrance to her throat. Her body shook in protest and her throat emitted a "gaaaaaaa!" sound. Drabik pressed on and he lodged his cock in Anya's throat.

The haughty and beautiful pirate's daughter shook and moaned as she felt the thick meat lodge in her esophagus. Drabik laughed as he felt the tight constriction of her membranes and saw her body shake and tremor. "This is how a ponygirl sucks cock, Anya. Do you like it?" he taunted her.

He waited until Anya's frantic reactions bordered on panic and then he slowly withdrew it just enough so that the unhappy woman could draw air. She took a lungful and he pushed his manhood back into its lodgment. For ten minutes, he worked Anya's throat. "Don't bite me now, lover, or I'll have to cut your throat. You wouldn't want that, would you?" he instructed her, his voice ominous.

Anya only reply was a desperate moan as she felt her throat widened each time the hot meat was pressed home. Twice, she tried to speak, uttering mumbled protests over Drabik's stiff rod. But she was literally wasting her breath as Drabik maintained the steady, slow pistoning of his cock. Her whole body would convulse as her need for air doubled until the next withdrawal.

The callous slave trainer was waiting for the moment where Anya would accept the presence of his thick prick without struggle. It was much like the taming of a pony, in fact, just like it, as the pony needed to accept her master's dominance and control of her body. "Relax, Anya," he said to her, "let it happen. Enjoy it."

Gradually, reluctantly, the tall, black haired beauty began to accommodate the invasive tool. Her long, white graceful legs, although still tense and quivering, ceased their testing of her bonds. Her body stilled. The man gave her mouth and throat several long, languid strokes of his cock. Although she shuddered each time that the prick plowed past her throat's entrance, she passively accepted it.

The girl was stunned with Drabik's outrageous abuse of her body. Her mind rebelled against the thick hard rod that was pressing into her inner space, blocking her airway. Her stomach was nauseous as her tongue was pressed down in her mouth and her narrow tube in her throat widened with each of Drabik's deliberate strokes. But when her lover had urged her to accept the inevitable, to cease resistance to his will, she closed her mind to her impulses and let the stiff manhood have its way with her.

Drabik had rested his hands to either side of Anya's shoulders while he was teaching her the basics of throat fucking. But now that he had forced her into a reluctant acceptance of his will, he took his hands and placed them on her large, chalk white breasts. He began to massage them as he continued to probe the woman's throat. Anya's body seemed to almost melt in front of him as it registered the effects of his attentions.

When he saw her lustful reaction, Drabik leaned forwards and, extending his legs, placed his head between her thighs. He took her pleasure bud between his lips and sucked on it gently, maintaining his cock's relentless steady pace. Anya's body jolted as if electrified and she began to moan with excited passion. It took only a few moments and her hips were bucking and thrusting, her passion overflowing its boundaries. Her tongue and lips began to work Drabik's cock as it passed through her mouth. "Uuugh! Uuugh!" she called out as her orgasm over took her.

The ponygirl trainer's lust was ready to peak as well. He could feel his balls tightening and his cock filling with his seminal fluid. He quickly regained his knees, abandoning Anya's stiff clit. He held the still moaning woman's head still with his hands, pressing them on either side of her cheeks and jaw, forcing the mouth to remain open to receive his discharge. He pulled his cock back until the head was lying on the roof of her mouth. He wanted the proud lady of the manor to taste his spunk. His cock began to pump his seed into her. When Anya realized what was happening, she protested and squirmed, trying to free her head from Drabik's mighty grasp. But jet after jet of his cum poured into her mouth and over her tongue. "Nuuuuuh! Nuuuuuh!" she tried to communicate her disapproval. But her voice was stilled as her cavity filled with Drabik's hot fluid.

Drabik groaned with sexual satisfaction as his cock throbbed and jerked in Anya's mouth. When the last spasm sent its load inside her, Drabik withdrew his prick and put his hand over her mouth. "A good ponygirl swallows her master's jism, Anya," he told her, his voice laden with sarcasm. "Take a good swallow now and enjoy its distinctive flavor. You're going to have to get to like it if you're going to suck cock like a ponygirl."

Anya gave in to the inevitable. It was better than letting the slimy substance lay dormant in her mouth. As it went down, her stomach turned.

Drabik waited until he saw calmness return to Anya's face. He released his hand expecting a torrent of abuse. Anya looked at him, towering above him. "Oh, Anton," she said, her voice exuberant. "I've never come like that before, that was incredible! And I could feel your cock down my throat, it was, …oh. I can't describe it!" Her face was bright with the residue of her ecstasy.

The man rolled over and poured himself another shot of vodka. He drank it in one gulp. "You liked it?" he asked, gruffly, not surprised that even a spoiled, proud women like Anya enjoyed being treated like a whore. He leaned over her, grabbing her heavy, breasts in his hands, massaging them.

"It was indescribable, Anton," she told him. "But please untie me now. I want to get loose," she asked plaintively.

"Oh, no, Anya, I can't do that," he replied. He pinched her nipples harshly, making the pretty, black haired girl moan. He grinned at her. "As soon as my cock gets hard again," he told her, "I'm going to fuck your cunt."

CHAPTER SEVEN

The sound of the tack room door slamming shut woke the splayed ponygirl. It took Maddy a few moments to realize where she was. A heavyset, black bearded man dressed in denim work clothes appeared in front of her. Viewing him with her head back made him appear upside down. He looked surprised to see her and then shrugged his shoulders. He went behind the counter where the leather goods were stored and fussed around for a few moments. He then returned to Maddy and contemplated the invitation issued by her widespread legs and her naked, hairless cunt. Maddy felt him step between her legs and place his hand on her pudendum. Her vulva was still sore from Drabik's beating and she jumped at his touch.

The ponygirl was thirsty and hungry. Her neck was sore from its unusual positioning and her back ached where it was lying on her bound wrists beneath her. She nevertheless felt a tingle in her loins as the man used his thumb to excite the small bud that lay at the apex of her sex. The discs attached to the rings in her labia jingled as he manipulated her swollen purse. Once she had begun to lubricate, the man started sliding his thumb between her nether lips and probing deeper and deeper into her womb. When he was satisfied that she was moist and loose enough, he withdrew his cock from his pants and inserted it inside her.

As the cock slid home, Maddy sighed. She had no power to fight the man's callous use of her, and little will to try. Her mind concentrated on the pleasurable feelings of having the man's rigid sex inside her, driving out the aches and pains. As the man continued to pump his pole into her welcoming chasm, Maddy felt her pussy grow warm and her body begin to respond to his efforts. But before she could get up a head of steam, she heard the man grunt and moan. She felt his spunk flood her tunnel. When he withdrew, Maddy groaned in frustration.

The tack room was usually busy in the mornings. Stable boys and trainers would come in looking for this or that, trying to get a buckle or belt repaired. The tack room manager had moved Maddy's cart so that she was in front of the counter and her feet faced the door. She could hear the men come and go but not see them. They would joke about the splayed pony and absentmindedly stroke her sex or her breasts while they spoke to the manager. Two of the men took advantage of her widespread legs to plow her furrow, spilling their seed inside her. Only one of the men brought her to orgasm and that was with his hand as he watched her body spasm and jerk with passion.

Outside of the ponygirl barn, Vadym was beside himself. Where was Lightning? She had not been checked into a stall the night before. It was unlikely, but not impossible that she had somehow been left unattended and scampered off; some of the ponies had tried it. If so, she would not get far. Any local resident would return an escaped pony to her master with the certainty of reward. They would consider it within their rights to make full use of her first.

There was the more real possibility that she had been stolen. There is no honor among thieves and any of Grobgy's rivals would be pleased to deprive him of a freshly trained racing pony. They would not be able to race her because Grobgy's mark of ownership was clearly set forth on her body. It was enough that Grobgy would be deprived of her use. Also, she could still be used for pulling a cart around the countryside and for carnal pleasures.

Persephone stood outside the barn tethered to a post while Vadym paced. She, of course, had no idea why he was so frustrated and could not understand the invectives he poured on the stable manager. Finally, at about 10:30, one of the trainers who was passing heard someone mention that Lightning was missing and told them that she was in the tack room. Vadym cursed and swore when he saw her bound body displayed on the mounting cart. She was covered in red stripes from Drabik's whip and a man was standing between her legs pumping his cock into her. Vadym went ballistic and screamed and shouted at the man, putting him off of his stroke. He withdrew without discharging, his stiff cock pointed at the ceiling. Vadym ordered the stable boy that had come with him to unfasten her from her perch and to bring her with them.

Maddy was disappointed when she felt the hot cock leave her pussy. She was also frightened because she heard Vadym's ranting. She remembered his voice from the day before. Last night, when she had been alone in the dark, awaiting sleep as a deliverance, she had wished that he would come and take her away. But now, hearing his angry voice, she was not so sure. Would she be going out of the frying pan into the fire?

The pony's body was lifted from the cart and she was set on her feet. A leash was attached to her nose ring and she was led out of the tack room. Maddy expected to be taken to the barn at least to be cleaned and fed. But she felt herself pulled in the opposite direction. They passed the track and walked along a pathway that Maddy had not been on before. The furthest from the barn she had been since her arrival was when she was taken to be tattooed and pierced. And that was no more than a hundred and fifty yards off of the beaten path. She continued walking behind the stable boy for a long time. She wanted to turn her head back and forth so that she could appreciate her surroundings, but the tension of the leash on her nose ring and her tiny eye holes kept her view straight ahead. They were on the other side of the big house, that she could tell. There were flower beds and a great lawn. The barns and the training track were faced with the back of Grobgy's mansion. Now Maddy was seeing its front, with wide, white, wooden steps leading up to a broad veranda. There was a broad stone walkway that led up to the house. Maddy was led past the front of the dacha and towards the other side. There, down a small hill, was a large, expansive plain. On it was a modern racing track around a bright green, well trimmed lawn. There were stands on one side of the track with a podium and a reviewing box. About two hundred yards from the track were a series of large trailers. Around the trailers there were all kinds of activities: ponies pulling carts towards the track, men walking to and fro. Naked women seemed to be scurrying around busily. Maddy's view was restricted and so she could not take in the panorama, but she knew that it dwarfed the training areas in which she had spent many weeks.

Vadym and the stable boy led her past the track and over to the trailers. She was taken to a large brown and white trailer that was hooked up to a dark blue pick up truck. As she came closer, she could see that her cart mate was already there, tethered to a hook on the rear of the trailer. She would know those fine breasts anywhere. She wore a blue and gold hood over her face.

A naked young woman wearing leather bracelets around her wrists and ankles came running up. She was wearing one of the face shield gags that the ponies wore when not in their bridles and bits. She had long, blond, stringy hair. Her nether lips were shaved and she wore on her stomach a tattoo of a large brown bear, its paws over its head and a cruel grimace on its face, showing its large fangs. This was the mark of one of the number of slave training facilities around the country. Slaves, whether purchased at wholesale rates from Khalid or one of the other dealers, or brought there by a private owner, were always sent to a training facility before being licensed to be released to the 'discrete' public. Intensive medical checks were made and intensive lessons in obedience and compliance were taught. Each training facility has its distinctive mark and the one that this shapely young woman had been brought to used a raging bear as its emblem. Other emblems used by other facilities include a snarling boar's head, a coiled python and a black falcon, its wings extended and its talons poised to strike. The slave girls also wear, emblazoned across their upper chests, tattooed, Cyrillic letters representing the new names they were provided with while in training.

The young woman bowed to her master with a lowering of her head and the bending of her knees, halfway between a full bow and a curtsey. She took the leash from the stable boy who was waved away by Vadym. Maddy did not know it, but she was to be Vadym's ward for the next seven weeks. She would undergo an additional week's worth of training and then six weeks of bi-weekly competitions, culminating, hopefully, in the National Tournament. Ponies, or individual pony teams, had to acquire a certain number of points over the six week racing season to be invited to race in the Nationals. The Tournament was held like any regular track event with a paddock and stands and betting booths. The standard race meet would involve up to seven ponies or teams of ponies. On the circuit, the racing facilities varied greatly in quality and usually were conducted as head to head or sometimes three way competitions between estate teams. The non-official "National Commission" set the schedules to establish parity and competitiveness. There were at least thirty estates that fielded teams and you could not race them all in a season. So the matchups had to consider evenness of competition so that one team would not breeze to the Nationals after sweeping an easy field and the others have to claw their way there fighting one good team after another. At some of the local meets, the smaller estates would be permitted to run individual events, but the larger estates were required to field a full team in order to compete.

All of this seems quite fantastic, and it is. But it must be recalled that Kalikastan is mostly closed to international visitors except with a special permit and then only within a small radius of Dlitski. The racing takes place within a defined area in the interior. Simple corruption, combined with the country's strategic importance, forestall any international scandal. Not that word of the sport hasn't spread. There had been bids from some African and Latin American teams for racing credentials. Also, some of the other former Soviet states have rekindled the sport within their domains and there has been talk of international competitions. Last year a Bolivian team was allowed in to run in some pre-season exhibitions.

The track that Maddy had seen on her way to Vadym's trailer was the competition track, as opposed to the training track where Maddy had first learned her trade. It was meticulously maintained and Maddy would find that running on it was a distinct pleasure. Its track was well groomed and with just the right hardness to allow the running of many teams over it in the course of a meet, but soft enough so that a pony could get real traction while churning to top speed.

The naked girl led Maddy to the side of the trailer. There was a table set up with a large pot of porridge steaming on a gas burner. The girl urged Maddy to her knees. The table was set within an enclosure made of tall blue and yellow fabric panels so that no one could view what happened inside. Maddy saw the slave girl ladle a large spoonful of the porridge into a bowl. She then dripped a stream of golden honey into it. She placed the bowl on the ground in front of Maddy and unbuckled Maddy's gag. The pony looked down at the steaming bowl and could smell the honey as it wafted up to her nostrils. Without a word, but with a slight smile of anticipation, she leaned over and placed her mouth in the bowl.

The sweet taste of the honey was like heaven to her. She consumed the hot porridge with glee. She didn't care if her new master beat her all day as long as he allowed her to eat this well. She would suck his cock for hours if he wanted.

Maddy licked the entire bowl clean. The girl pulled her to her feet and brought her to a shower head running from the side of the trailer. She turned it on and delightfully warm water poured over the happy pony. The girl was shorter than the pony and she had to reach up to wash her neck and shoulders. The slave girl washed her body clean, being careful to delve into her abused slit and between the cheeks of her hindquarters. The water had stung at first as it came into contact with Maddy's many wounds from the night before. But she got used to it quickly enough.

After washing her body, the girl had Maddy kneel. She had a bowl of hot water and a shaving brush. Maddy knew that her head and sex would be shaved next. The girl laid her hand on the side of Maddy's face and looked into her eyes. Although Maddy could not see her facial expression due to the sheath over the bottom portion, she felt compassion from the girl, the first time that she had felt it for almost two months. Tears welled up in her eyes. She moved her lips to form a word and the girl quickly put her hand over them, her eyes alarmed. She looked around to make sure no one was watching and then wagged her finger at the kneeling pony.

Standing behind her, the slave girl removed her stretchy, blue hood. Maddy felt the girl apply the shaving soap to her scalp. She usually dreaded her daily shave, but today she relaxed and enjoyed the touch of the sympathetic, young slave girl's hands. When her head was again free of any stubble, and after applying the antiseptic ointment, the girl used a washcloth to clean her pale white face, a face that no one had seen for many weeks. After her face was cleaned, the girl applied a soothing lotion to keep the skin soft and moist.

The girl then adorned Maddy's head with a new, clean hood. She felt the girl bind her tail and then pass it through the hole in the back. Her hood, like Persephone's was divided into blue and gold panels, with the right side of her head being gold and the left blue. These were Grobgy's racing colors, and the ponies would wear them until the spring racing season was over. It helped the punters identify the ponies as they watched the morning exercises before the races, hoping to get a betting edge. It also instilled pride in the teams who saw that they were being treated as a sort of pony royalty. When a pony was let off the team due to poor performance or serious injury, the loss of this status symbol was keenly felt.

After connecting the bottom of the hood to the pony's collar, the slave girl washed Maddy's long ponytail, dried it with a towel and then brushed it with at least twenty five strokes. Maddy enjoyed the gentle tugs on her head as the brush descended down the long, auburn strands.

The girl gently laid a bridle over Maddy's head and installed the dreaded bit in her mouth. She patted her on the head and brought her to her feet. Maddy felt cleaner than she had in weeks. It was not that she had not been well taken care of in the pony barn, but this al fresco shower and the gentle treatment of the girl made her feel refreshed and, well, clean.

The girl took out a tube of lotion, a skin softener, and began to rub it all over Maddy's body. Maddy sighed as the girl's hands found all of her sensual places, lingering there as she rubbed the lotion in. Her legs were spread apart and the girl got on her knees and rubbed the inside of her thighs. When she was done, she stood next to the pony's delightfully tingling body and laid her own naked torso against it. The slave girl came up to the tip of Maddy's nose and she could smell the girl's fresh scent in her hair. The girl's breasts lay softly against Maddy's skin, her own more ample globes resting atop them. Maddy felt the girl's hand trace across her tattooed stomach and descend to her hairless mound. Her delicate fingers teased Maddy's labia, causing a rush of passion to course through the pony's body. Her fingers pried the nether lips apart and delved in between, coaxing Maddy's wetness. The girl raised her head to Maddy. Her star blue eyes, set above her leather mask, telegraphed her yearning for Maddy's flesh.

Just when Maddy began to sigh and moan in pleasure, the girl ceased her manipulation of Maddy's wet pussy. She stepped quickly over to the trailer and picked up the leash that Maddy had worn when brought there, attached it to her golden nose ring and led her from the shielded glade to the rear of the van. There Maddy joined her partner, Persephone, who was waiting patiently for her.

After about a half hour, Vadym came walking up the path. Behind him two ponies were pulling a bright, shiny cart. The seat was a distinctive brown leather and the brass frame was burnished a golden yellow. The shafts were of fine, new wood, stained a deep brown and lacquered to make them shine. The wheels were painted half yellow and half blue. A pennant hung in the air behind the carriage mounted on a strong, thin wire.

This was the racing cart, and to Maddy and Persephone, it appeared miraculously wonderful. They were beginning to get a sense of the special role they were about to play and the importance that their performance would mean to the estate. In a way, it was thrilling to them, for so little special had happened to them since their kidnappings. But on the other hand, failure bespoke special, cruel punishments. They would strive to do their best.

Maddy and Persephone were worked hard that day by Vadym. He gave both of their legs extensive massages prior to taking them out, making sure that their muscles were warm and loose. They trotted at a leisurely pace for a few laps. And then Vadym made them show him what they could really do. The ponies dug deep into the track to propel themselves along it. Their thighs pumped furiously in unison as they sped along. Vadym carefully pulled them back from their top speed, not wanting to strain them, satisfied with their handling and their performance. When they were led down to the trailer for lunch, sweaty and tired, he rewarded both of them with a small piece of chocolate slipped over their bits.

The ponies were showered and fed. There was a toilet facility that served the entire camp area and the ponies were taken there for relief. The slave girl brushed them down and then fed them. They were fed in separately screened areas lest they see each other's faces, an event that would have been taken with sincere displeasure. It was also considered bad luck.

In the camp area with Maddy and Persephone were the estate's other racing teams. There was the troika team, the four pony chaise team, the six pony cabriolet and the nine pony landaus. Then there were the sulkies. These were one pony carts, the Alfa Romeo's of the sport. There were two sulky races, the 1500 and the 3000 meter. The ponies that pulled them were the crème de la crème of racing ponies, sleek, strong ponies, fast and agile, without a trace of fat on them. They were treated as the thoroughbreds that they were. They were driven by special small, light jockeys, with no weight limits. The matching of a driver with a sulky pony was a delicate thing since the carriage itself was so light. Unless carefully balanced with the jockey's weight, it could flip over on turns.

Maddy and Persephone ran a few laps in the afternoon, but what Vadym worked on especially was their start. They must have dashed off of the line twenty five times that afternoon. At one point, Vadym became so upset with their imprecise starts that he whipped their bottoms with a light pony whip. The whippings did not hurt as much as the disappointment they felt for failing to come up to snuff. Vadym tied a rope between their right thighs, just above their knees. As they pulled from the starting line, their legs instantly communicated their motion to each other. After ten tries, they finally got it right, digging their right feet deep down into the turf at exactly the same time and with exactly the same force. When they were done, he gave them another candy.

After the ponies were rubbed down on a special table set up by the slave girl while they were exercising, they were showered and fed. The rub downs were done by Vadym himself. His strong hands carefully teased their muscles, churning the blood in them, popping out any knots. Their hands were unhitched from behind their backs and chained to the top of the table and their collars were removed so that Vadym could get at their backs and necks. He finished each session by dipping his head between their widespread thighs and slowly and softly caressing them to climax with his lips and tongue. Their bodies were so relaxed that when they came, it was more of a mesmerizing throb of delight, which made their bodies tremble, rather than an earth shattering orgasm.

After dinner, the ponies were left to sit and play. They were permitted to lean against one another and use their thighs to rub each other's pussies. The slave girl would stroke them to orgasm several times. On alternate nights, one of them would be allowed to suck Vadym's cock to orgasm, kneeling between his legs as he sat in his comfortable folding chair. Maddy loved the feel of his cock in her mouth and would prolong and delay his climax until he could stand it no more and pushed her head down on his throbbing pole, plunging it into her throat.

Vadym never fucked them and the ponies missed having their lower orifices filled. But when he was happy with their training day, he would have the slave girl spread a blanket on the grass, remove the ponies' gags and let them kiss and pleasure each other. He would sit and smoke while Maddy and Persephone, lovers who had never seen each other's faces and who had no knowledge of each other's names, dipped their heads between each other's thighs and brought each other to pleasure. Persephone had a long, active tongue and she would tickle Maddy's clit while Maddy lay on her back with her legs spread. Then she would push her tongue deep within her slit, drawing moans and sighs from her partner. Although their mouths were ungagged while they enjoyed their reward, neither pony ventured to utter one word, so used had they become to the prohibition and so unhappy they would have been to incur their driver's displeasure.

None of the other trainers or drivers were allowed to touch the racing ponies during the season. Grobgy would lend a few of the house slaves to the trainers during this period and would rent a few more from a nearby brothel to satisfy their carnal needs. Those girls would get a taste of pony life, as they were held in the otherwise empty pony stalls, gagged and hooded, when not in actual use.

And there were the house ponies, the ones used for pleasure and mere transportation. They would always know when pony racing season had started by the dramatic increase in their sexual activity.

During the ten days before the first race, Grobgy came by twice to the little trailer park to review his racing stable. He was at the rail at the track daily, timing ponies, watching their handling. Maddy cringed when she saw him for it was a stark reminder that she was still his property. She did not know when she would actually race, how long the season would last or anything about their schedule. But she knew that sooner or later she would be back in the pony barn. The way that her owner looked at her as she knelt before him while he talked to Vadym told her that someday soon he would take a more physical possession of her. She feared the fierce looking bandit and his deadly cold black eyes.

And she feared the lady who she assumed was his daughter, the one who had cruelly egged her trainer on to abuse her. She watched the ponies on an almost daily basis as well. Once she had come to the camp. Her eyes remained glued to Maddy as she laughed and joked with Vadym.

And then there was her trainer, the man she thought of as her master. While he did not make an appearance, he was almost always present in her mind. He had treated her brutally the last time she had seen him and she had no reason to believe that he was not waiting for her, biding his time to bring her more punishing torment for sins that she did not know that she committed.

Finally, it was the night before the first match. The opposing racing team had arrived during the day in their trailers and trucks. There was a large camping area set aside for them. Maddy saw the ponies from the other team cruising the track in the late afternoon, getting used to its footing. Their hoods were bright red and their carriages were decorated similarly. They looked strong and confident. Maddy's stomach grew queasy as she worried how well she and her sister pony would perform.

That night there was a huge banquet at the mansion. Opening day was the event of the season and people had come from miles around. The ponygirls of both teams had been installed on either side of the long driveway, tethered to posts, wearing their racing hoods, red team on the right and blue and gold on the left. It was a little before dusk on this mid-May evening when the guests started to arrive. A long line of dark limousines and black Mercedes edged its way from the distant main road to the front steps of the mansion. Some of the guests arrived on pony carts of their own, all bedecked with finery, and much fanfare was made of them.

The passengers and drivers leaned out of their windows to gawk at the naked ponygirls. Torches had been set into the ground on tall poles and one of Grobgy's minions came down the line lighting them. The ponies were tethered by the back of their collars to the posts and their ankles were set wide apart and connected to steel rings hammered into the ground. The result saw them posed as if a still life, with their legs apart and their shaven sexes and pierced loins exposed. Their masters' logos could be seen prominently displayed on their bellies.

The red team belonged to a gangster originally from Minsk. He had looted several of the major banks established after the fall of the former Soviet Union and now he collected ponygirls and served as a banker for many of the underworld schemes that sprung up in this Wild West type nation. His loans were backed up by the enforcement powers of one of the more lethal and powerful clans. If you owed money to Pieter Njinsky, you paid him.

Njinsky had adopted the fox as his herald. It was a brilliant design with red fangs and a gray and brown fur coat. His motto was emblazoned beneath the fearsome engraving, "Fortes Fortuna Juvat" - fortune favors the bold. His team had not raced here before and this was the first chance that many of the guests had had to see his trademark tattoo up close. They rubbed their hands across the bellies of the nervous ponies and made appreciative remarks.

The names and specialties of the ponies, i.e. sulky, chaise, pony cart, et cetera, as well as their nationality and "birthdate", meaning their date of acquisition, were printed on a cardboard sign implanted in the ground next to them. Many of the guests remarked on Maddy's recent conversion from human being to pony and wondered if she would "have what it takes" to run well the next day. Persephone had been a ponygirl for five months, having been converted in December of the prior year. Both of the other team's yearlings had been taken in January.

Training for Grobgy's ponies during the winter months took place in a huge indoor facility outside the capital. There were several around the nation, and ponygirls were lodged there for the winter months. While there, they received regular attention, both by way of exercise and of sexual use. Persephone had begun her training there months before Maddy had come to Grobgy's estate, but Maddy had been a quick study and, it was generally agreed, was ready to be raced.

There was a long cocktail hour before dinner and the guests leisurely walked the line of hooded, faceless ponygirls mounted along the driveway, drinks in hand, admiring their qualities. Maddy was appallingly embarrassed to be thus displayed before the clearly wealthy and sophisticated crowd. She could see them, dressed in the best summer fashions, through the small holes of her hood as they passed by. Some would stop in front of her and talk about her as if she were not human and couldn't hear. She couldn't understand what they said, but it seemed horribly strange to her that so many people could blithely accept her reduction to an owned beast without qualm. It also served to remind her of something that she had somehow forgotten: there was an entire world outside the limits of the estate on which she was being held prisoner, a world of cars and parties and pretty dresses, a world where women roamed free.

She reddened as a young girl, not more than twenty, accompanied by her older lover, approached. She was clearly impressed with Maddy's nose ring and labial piercings. She was dressed in a frilly white dress with short sleeves and a deep, plunging neckline. She had pleasant, round breasts, and the sides of them could be seen quivering as she talked excitedly with her older companion. She had long, bare arms and dangled a cigarette out of one hand and held a drink in the other. Maddy couldn't remember the last time that she had had hands.

The young girl laughed and joked with her friend, a well dressed middle aged man. Maddy wondered if she was a whore. The girl must have sensed Maddy's approbation because she stepped up to her with a frown. Handing her drink to her friend and discarding her cigarette, she ran her hands over Maddy's breasts and pulled at her nose ring. "Amerikanski Molyna," Maddy heard. She had said her name. The young girl leaned over and whispered in her ear in heavily accented English, "See you tomorrow, ponygirl." She laughed and walked away.

It was strange for Maddy to hear English spoken after all these weeks. It reminded her that she did in fact have a language and that she once spoke many times in a single day. And it reminded her that she was not always a naked, shaved beast fit for display to the decadent rich. She became self conscious of her nakedness. Unconsciously, she tried to move her feet together, but the binding on her ankles held firm. She realized that her nationality must be on the placard planted next to her. She wondered what other information it contained. Was there any chance that someone who saw that a young American girl was being held prisoner as a ponygirl would contact someone? At once, Maddy realized the impossibility of that. No one who was a threat to these people would be invited to a party where the ponies were so brazenly displayed. It was a sign of her owner's indifference to the consequences that he would put her nationality on a sign next to her.

For the first time in a while, Maddy felt lonely and abandoned. Tears formed in her eyes, tears that no one would see since they were blocked by her hood. She yearned to be back at the trailer where life was simpler and she could forget that she was once named Madeline Burnham and that a cruel, strange fate had befallen her. She wanted life to be normal, to be next to her blond tailed lover and the kindly slave girl. She wanted to be on her knees between her driver's legs, his cock in her mouth, blocking out everything else around her.

Although touching of the ponies was discouraged, more than one woman, dressed languidly in a long, light summer gown, had tickled her nether lips until she became moist. They looked into her eye holes, seeking some reaction from the featureless creature. When she moaned in the preliminary stage of sexual excitement, they would laugh and walk away. One man, obviously already drunk, stepped up and kissed her nipple, taking it between his lips and sucking on it hard. His girlfriend pulled him away, her laughter covering her embarrassment.

Maddy stood out on the driveway until the dinner bell was rung at 8 p.m. Grooms from the estate came to collect the ponies. They were led to their trailers where their drivers were waiting. The ponies were fed and watered and their other needs seen to. Maddy and her sister pony were left hitched to the rear of the trailer. This seemed unusual to Maddy since by now she was usually getting set in for the night.

After standing for about an hour, she saw her driver emerge from the side of the trailer and that he was outfitted in a bright yellow satin shirt that buttoned up along the side of his chest. He wore shiny blue pants and had a yellow and blue cap on his head. He greeted his ponies with tender caresses of their breasts while the slave girl applied their harnesses. Maddy wondered if the races were going to start this very night, for she could think of no other explanation for being set in her harness at this dark hour. In addition to their harness, the slave girl mounted tall blue and yellow feathers to their hoods.

When she and Persephone were harnessed in place, Vadym took the reins and urged them softly forward. He steered them towards the track where a line of red and yellow and blue carriages were waiting. The night lights of the track were on.

Dinner was over at about 9:30, and the guests were all invited down to the race track for champagne and dessert. White gloved servants handed out glasses of champagne while naked slave girls carried trays of pastries and cookies. While not invited to the banquet, the trainers and stable boys, grooms and other workers whose jobs revolved around the ponygirls, were invited to partake in the merriment at the track. Drabik wandered through the crowd aimlessly. He abjured the flinty champagne and yearned for a shot of hot vodka. He saw Anya flirting with a tall handsome guest wearing a finely tailored tuxedo. He would make her pay for that, he thought. Since the night he had taught her to throat fuck, their sessions together had become more and more outré. He always brought something to tie her hands with, and she now had learned to service his cock from her knees, hands bound behind her, drinking down every drop of cum that he spilled.

There was a flare from a trumpet and the guests hurriedly found their seats in the grandstand. Grobgy and Nijinsky and their most honored guests sat in the reviewing box. A brass ensemble had been playing and now they approached a set of microphones. After a moment's pause, they broke out into a long, excited flourish and then began to play a brilliant, Soviet era march.

The flourish was the signal for the patiently awaiting drivers. The lead ponies were started and the column of red and blue and yellow bedecked carriages began to slowly crawl towards the track. They entered the track on the far side, chaises first, and they commenced a slow steady pace around it. The crowd was in great humor as the brightly decorated ponygirls drew the carriages expertly towards them. When the lead carriage, drawn by four beautiful, large breasted ponygirls entered the stretch, the crowd became excited. The lead set of ponygirls was from Grobgy's team as he was the host of the meet. When the ponies reached the beginning of the grand stand, their driver snapped their reins and they began a stylish canter, knees raised high, each step deliberate and precise. Their breasts bobbed and weaved as they marched, the lights gleaming off of their highly polished, black boots, their plumes waving in the wind. As the phaetons passed the reviewing box, the drivers doffed their caps and saluted the owners and their special guests.

After the four ponied chaises came the six ponied cabriolets. The cabriolets by rule contained a driver and passenger. Their combined weights were strictly governed by regulation. They were not as fast as the chaises, but required twice as much strength to pull. Following the phaetons were the troikas, each carriage sporting a trio of finely trained ponies. Each set of ponies cantered jauntily for the benefit of the crowd. Cheers went up as each carriage began its demonstration of its ponies' discipline, training and skill. The fact that naked, servile females who had been stolen from their homes and stripped of their humanity were prancing before them, their graceful, well trimmed bodies and their gorgeous naked breasts displayed for all to see, was not lost on the excited crowd.

Grobgy was beside himself with pride, pride of ownership and pride of his own exalted status. He had licked the boots of many of his superiors in the Soviet security apparatus. Later he had shot some of them. All had seemed lost when the red Army tanks refused to crush the defenders of the Russian White House that day years ago. Within months the Soviet Union had dissolved and the Communist Party of the Soviet Union was banned. It took two more years of maneuvering and intrigue, but with the Yeltsin counterrevolution of 1993, Grobgy and his former KGB friends were back on top. Ministries were handed out like soda pop and the right to control factories and industries often grew out of the barrel of a gun. That was a sea he could swim in and, in a few years, he had amassed a huge fortune. Unfortunate interference by so called reformers had mandated his dejure banishment from the new Russian Republic, but the even newer, sovereign nation of Kalikastan provided a safe haven, and since then his defatco control of power and money inside his former homeland continued.

He watched with self satisfaction as every other cart was pulled by servile, former women owned by him. He held the power of life and death over them and their sister slaves who populated the great house. And he carried that power over many others who would perish if their conduct compromised one of his 'projects'. Through assassins like Drabik, he was able to project his will deep into Russia and other neighboring countries. Lenin had electricity and the soviets as the basis for Bolshevik power. He had cash and bullets.

Maddy and Persephone followed the troikas. They had been practicing their cantering for several days. It had been learned weeks earlier at the point of a 2" round cane. Now they proudly lifted their knees in unison and began their studied gait past the grand stand. The excitement of the moment was not lost on them. In a world where their ability to forecast future events was virtually nil, to know what tomorrow would bring was a new experience. Tomorrow was race day, and as Maddy cantered in unison with her sister pony past their owner's reviewing box, her breasts heaving on her chest, her heart pounding in her ears, she yearned for success.

Last to proceed past the reviewing box were the sulkies. Each team carried two sulkies, one for the 1500 meters and the other for the 3000. A pony needed speed for the first and speed and strength for the second. While some aficionados of the sport value the 1500 meter sprint as the gold cup race of the sport, those with a true knowledge of the fundamentals of pony racing treasure the swift endurance needed for the 3000. It was for this reason that the 3000 meter sulkies closed the parade and for this reason that the 3000 was always the last race of the day. The best was saved for last.

A pony that could pull a 3000 meter sulky at a world class pace was a true rara avis. Scouts were at work all over the western world looking for the right young female who might become a 3000 meter champion. Grobgy's 3000 meter sulky, Quicksilver, was a former long distance runner for UCLA. She had not been eminently successful as a long distance runner, for although she had the endurance, she did not have the speed. But Grobgy's scouts knew that foot speed alone meant little when you were hauling a 100 lb. carriage and a 90 to 100 lb, rider. One look at her in the University's weight room had sold them. In her junior year, she was invited to participate gratis in a summer physical fitness program in Finland. The brochure and web site made it seem so enticing, and it included a two week tour of European capitals, all expenses paid, plus scholarship money for her senior year. It was an offer that she should have, but could not, pass up. She was met at the airport at Helsinki by a friendly limousine driver. An hour later she was across the Russian border.

It had taken Quicksilver two years to break into the upper ranks of 3000 meter sulkies. But this year she was in top form and expected to take first place at the Spring Tournament. As she cantered past the reviewing box, the crowd gave a raucous cheer. They knew a great champion when they saw one.

CHAPTER EIGHT

Jake had been in Kalikastan for about three weeks when Burnham flew in. He met him at the airport and had a car waiting. Burnham was all business.

"Is the meeting all set up?" he asked.

"It's all set up," Jake answered. "It's at 9 tonight. I've got us a little place outside of the city. I've had it swept so it'll be okay to talk there."

"Any bugs?"

"Of course. There were the ones they knew we'd find, and then the other ones. It's clean, I'm sure," Jake told him.

"So who's there now?" Burnham asked.

"I've got Leon and Curly there. Martinez is doing some snooping around for me and this is Tucker, driving. I don't think you've met."

Tucker, a blockbuster kind of guy looked up into the rear view window and nodded. To say that Tucker was taciturn would be to overstate his eloquence. He spoke mostly with his meat cleaver sized hands.

The traffic on the only road from the airport was a cacophony of reckless vehicles going every which way. Three times the big, black Lincoln swerved, pushing Jake and Burnham onto each other in the back seat. After five or so Grand Prix type miles, the traffic ground to a virtual stop. There was a choke point where the airport traffic entered the city and the men spent a long time inching forwards.

Burnham looked around at the car. "Why a Lincoln?" he asked.

"Why not," Jake inquired.

"Because a Mercedes is about 200% more comfortable."

"Well," Jake answered, "this is the way I see it. We're Americans, everybody knows that. We're not going to get anywhere by pretending we're Germans, or British or anything else. We've got to come on strong and confident. So we drive an American car, perhaps <u>the</u> American car. Besides, it's easier to follow."

Burnham quickly looked behind them and peered out the back window. "Followed? We're being followed?"

"Of course," Jake answered.

Burnham, a 55 year old tall and trim man, had short black hair, meticulously groomed, a suave face and broad shoulders. Thirty years ago he would have mixed it up with any guy in any bar in America. But then he got filthy rich. He had scooped up in a bankruptcy sale a patent to a key component in personal computer systems, all of them. The part, an electronic chip that regulates the flow of electrons to the coprocessor, was cheap to make and was apparently the only way to make the damn things work at over 200 mgz. A markup of $7.50 for every computer made in the U.S., and Japan too, and, well, you get the picture. His patent infringement claim against the Chinese government was still pending with the State Department. Rumor had it that an exchange of stock was in the works. From computer chips, he had branched out to a wide variety of investments, from a huge international construction company to an Angola diamond mine. He had vast wealth, but he didn't have what was most precious to him of all, Madeline, his niece.

He was stunned by Jake's casual acceptance of their being tailed. "What do you mean, 'Of course'?" he asked Jake, ready to rip a bumbling employee a new asshole.

"Listen, Mr. Burnham," Jake answered, a slight hint of annoyance in his voice, "they're going to watch us no matter what we do. In fact, there's more than one group of folks interested in what we're doing. You want we should do one of those 'French Connection' scenes right here in Dlitski? First of all, Tucker doesn't know the city so every few blocks we'd have to stop and get directions. Second, we'd be liable to run somebody over and that somebody would be related to a guy related to a guy related to a guy, you know what I mean? And third, we've got nothing to hide. Everything's above board. You've got a visa, I've got a visa, I've got a residence permit, you've got a residence permit. And tonight we're meeting with the Minister of Trade, who's a member of, let's call it 'the Chamber of Commerce Round Table', a kind of commission that settles gang disputes. Also there will be the Minister of the Interior (read: secret police), and the undersecretary of a relatively obscure agency called the Ministry of Strategic Imports. He regulates the slave trade. And we're slavers, remember?"

Burnham was not used to employees talking to him this way. He was speechless. But then he reminded himself that Jake was not an employee, he was a contract hire, a specialist, and getting results was his main product.

"Okay," he conceded, not something he did that often, "I see your point." He looked around the car. "Where is all of this traffic coming from?" he asked.

"There are three highways narrowing down to two lanes up there."

"What?" Burnham exclaimed. "What's that all about?"

"Well it's another reason we don't need to shake our tail. Nobody gets in to Dlitski or out of it without permission. Everybody's got to show a pass."

"I didn't realize that internal security was so tight?" Burnham said.

"It's tight all right. It has to be. There about 5000 young ladies in the country who would like to be someplace else, about half of them in the city. There's all kinds of smuggling going on, most of it government sponsored or approved, and everybody needs to keep an eye on everybody else or else there'd be civil war, or a gang war anyway."

"Jeeze!" was all Burnham said.

* * * * * * * * * * * * * *

They pulled into the courtyard of a three story grey stuccoed building in a quiet residential section of the city. It had a red tile roof and tall, narrow windows in the front with black shutters. An elderly concierge with a bushy grey moustache and a peasant's cap opened the steel gate at the entrance so that the Lincoln could pass through. The house surrounded the courtyard on three sides. The grey day muted the colors of the large cobblestones and the gray exterior of the building. As Jake got out of the car, he noted a black Mercedes pull past the arched entrance and slide to a stop just beyond his vision. Their babysitters.

Leon, a wiry, lean man with short brown hair came out to greet them. Jake waved him off and went to the trunk to retrieve Burnham's bags. When they walked inside, Burnham looked wide eyed at the stylish, modern interior. "I expected neogothic," he said.

"And it's got all the most modern conveniences," Jake said in his mock estate agent voice.

The entrance foyer led to long hallway with maple wainscoting. They crossed the hall and entered a large living area with two long, pastel green couches set in an el and a large pale green oriental rug with a cream colored border in front of hem. There was a white oak bar at one end of the room and a stone fireplace at the other. Kneeling in the center of the room, their hands resting palms up on their widespread thighs were two naked, young women. They both had long, dirty blond hair and their pubic regions had been shaved leaving a small, wiry beard above their exposed slits. They bore on their taut bellies a tattoo of a green python, coiled, with snarling fangs and a long red tongue. They seemed like enough to be sisters. Even their breasts were matched sets of pale white, half grapefruits sitting high on their chests. Their eyes were downcast.

"What the fuck is this?" Burnham asked.

Jake put down the suitcases. "They came with the house."

"Bullshit," Burnham said, his eyes feasting on their pleasant forms.

"No, no bullshit," Jake replied. "There's two more upstairs."

"What are we supposed to do with them?" Burnham asked, obviously put off by the display of Kalikastan's main tourist attraction.

"You're supposed to fuck them, Mr. Burnham," Jake said, exasperated. "Listen, Mr. Burnham, I can't emphasize this enough. You're in a nasty business. You knew you would be when you started this thing. This," he pointed to the two young women, "is the end product of our little enterprise."

"You mean that these girls are from our…"

"No, Mr. Burnham, they're not ours," Jake replied cutting his employer off. "Ours haven't cleared training yet. We shipped our first lot about five weeks ago. Take a week off for breaking in at Khalid's, maybe a week for them to be selected by a retailer and four weeks of training. Our first girls should be coming out of the assembly line sometime next week. I can try and pick a couple up for you if you want."

"That won't be necessary, Jake," Burnham responded coldly. "Just tell me where I can get cleaned up and then we'll talk."

"Your bedroom is upstairs and to the left. It's the master bedroom. There's a slave girl in there. Her name is Peacock, or 'Pyacok' in Russian. She'll help you with your shower."

"I don't need help with my shower, Jake. I'm big boy now," Burnham replied as he headed for the stairs. He had his suitcase in his hand.

"Oh, you'll want the help when you see her, Mr. Burnham," Jake called up after him.

About an hour later, Burnham came down the stairs. He had changed from his grey, tailored business suit into a pair of light tan trousers with a yellow sports shirt and a brown herringbone sports jacket.

"How was the blow job, Mr. Burnham?" Leon asked, smiling.

"Never mind, asshole!" Burnham shot back. "Where's Jake?"

Leon tried to suppress a snigger. "In the shithouse," he said.

"When he comes out, I want to talk to him."

"Sure, Mr. Burnham," Leon responded. "Why don't you wait in the study, it's down the hall to the left."

Jake joined Burnham about ten minutes later. Burnham was looking out the narrow window that faced the street. "They're still out there," he said.

"Don't worry, Mr. Burnham, they won't bite."

"Okay, okay, Jake enough with the funny stuff. And tell your friend Leon I don't appreciate his humor."

"Listen, Mr. Burnham," Jake answered, just a degree below boiling, "these guys are here to protect your life. They're here risking theirs. Sure, they get paid a bundle, but they're worth it. You go tell Leon he has to mind his manners and he's on a plane back to St. Louis. And if he goes, you can kiss Curly goodbye because they always go together. And the...."

"All right, Jake, all right, I get the point. I'll just have to toughen my skin a little bit. "

"No problem, Mr. Burnham," Jake replied. He paused and started to smile. "By the way, how was the blowjob?"

Burnham leaked out a smile. "It was damn fine," he said. "Actually," he said, "I never experienced anything like it. It was if I was some kind of god to her. She..., well..., I mean I kept thinking that I could do anything I wanted to her. It was amazing."

"Just remember why we're here, Mr. Burnham," Jake told his boss. "Don't get carried away. It would be very easy for a man like you to get sucked in here. Try to remember that they are real people and that they aren't playing a game."

"I know why I'm here Jake," Burnham replied. "I don't need to be lectured."

"It's just that these people are expecting you to make a huge financial commitment here. Your money could be tied up here for many years. These guys aren't school boys. If you fuck with them, wherever you are and no matter how much protection you have, they'll get you one way or the other.

Burnham looked hard at Jake. "I am aware of everything you've said. Now let's get down to business."

The meeting was held at a small restaurant in the central part of the city. Martinez had been there for a few hours, checking out the security. It was purely a formality, since if the criminal rulers of this anarchic country wanted them dead, they would be dead.

The restaurant was called 'The Hideaway', and was decorated along the lines of an American twenties speakeasy. It was closed for the night for a 'private party'. When Jake and Burnham arrived, driven by Tucker and accompanied by Leon and Curly in a separate car, Martinez was at the door showing one of the local security men some of his knife tricks. He was a connoisseur with a knife, and he was flipping and dangling his 7" switchblade all around his body. The Kalikastani secret policeman responded by pulling out what looked like an 8" butcher's knife and tossing it across the street, embedded it in the trunk of a small, spruce sapling. Martinez whistled with admiration. He threw his knife and it landed about three inches higher on the tree. Both men laughed.

The entrance to the restaurant led down a set of winding stairs to a partially refinished cellar. There were twenty or so large round tables covered with red and white checkered tablecloths. Waxed over Chianti bottles sat on each one with partially melted candles set in their open necks. There were Rock Hudson and Doris Day movie posters on the walls. Jake had never seen a room filled with such mixed metaphors. They were waived towards a door in the rear of the restaurant by a short, fat bald headed man wearing a frayed tuxedo abut a size and a half too big for him. They proceeded through the doorway and found themselves in a small, modern room with salmon walls and a low, white ceiling. Along one wall, sitting on a raised dais, was a semicircular table. At it were sitting four men in business suits, all with short black hair and wearing stylish Italian suits. A fifth man sat at the end of the table. He was wearing a black turtle neck sweater and black pants. He had short, black, receding hair and wore round, wire rimmed glasses. Jake and Burnham were invited to take their places, Burnham in the middle of the four men, at the center of the table, Jake on the other end.

There were introductions all around and several toasts. Naked young women, their breasts decorated with little bells hanging from their nipples came out of the kitchen with large trays of delicacies. The women all bore a stylized red rose with small leaves surrounding it atop a thick thorny stem tattooed on their bellies and wore collars around their necks and thick leather bracelets around their wrists.

There was eel, pickled eggs, marinated goat, numerous cheeses, some dried beef sausages and a large assortment of olives and nuts. After three rounds of Vodka, several bottles of a locally grown wine were produced and served. It was dry, but with a fruity flavor, reminiscent of peaches. A new round of toasts followed. Each time Burnham tried to bring the conversation around to business, he was waved off and a new course of food was called for.

After a spicy beef dish served in a sour milk sauce was consumed by the group, the lights in the room flickered and a high pitched, zither type music began to flood the room. Their attention was drawn to a stage set on the wall opposite side them. A spotlight shown down on it, illuminating it fully. Suddenly, a line of beautiful young women, in actuality, the waitresses who had been serving them, came dancing out onto the stage. They were wearing short, black, diaphanous skirts that reached down to mid-thigh.

The girls quickly ran around the stage gracefully, their shoeless toes pointed, their bodies erect. When all five had entered the stage, they came together in the middle, their hands held high over their heads and brushed their bodies together. They were all very well endowed and their naked breasts rippled and swayed as they moved. Their eyes were lined with kohl and their succulent lips were painted blood red. They broke apart and assumed positions on the stage facing the banquet table, two in front and three staggered in the back so that all of the girls were clearly visible. They all wore the red and green rose tattoo on their bellies and when they started to move their hips to the music, the flowers began to jump and dance.

The young slave girls were moving slowly and languidly to the music. The stage was about fifteen feet from the banquet table and Jake and Burnham had an excellent view of the girls' assets. As the music encouraged them, the girls spread their hands over their bodies, proffering their pleasant, full breasts, running over their taut bellies and over their rounded hips. All the girls wore shoulder length hair that was loose and free on their heads and when they swayed their pretty necks, the hair followed suit, accentuating their graceful movements.

Suddenly, the music changed pace and four of the girls formed a semi-circle around a buxom blonde one. She smiled demurely at the dinner guests and slowly, her hips swaying to the leisurely beat, began to draw her short, translucent skirt down over her hips, past her knees and then to the floor. Her labia, imprisoned by a large golden lock that pierced them, were decorated with the same dark, blood red coloring as her lips. The inviting flesh was surrounded by a border of neatly trimmed, wiry blond hair.

The girl ran her hands along the sides of her sex and her face was posed in a seductive pout. She danced off of the stage and, her hips moving quickly to the staccato beat of the music, circled around the table and approached the millionaire. His eyes were glued to her gyrating pussy. She knelt beside him and, opening her mouth, stuck out her long, delicate tongue. On it sat a small, golden key. Burnham looked around him and, encouraged by the gestures of the Kalikastani hosts, gingerly lifted the key off of the girl's proffered tongue. She rose to her feet, her breasts dancing on her chest, her hips writhing frantically. She opened her legs and pushed her sex invitingly forwards. Burnham, looking nervous, took the key and undid the lock that pierced her nether lips. He carefully pulled the lock free of the holes in the girl's sex and looked up into the girl's face. She smiled at him and ran back to the stage.

One by one, the dancers freed themselves seductively from their dainty skirts and presented their loins to the American. Each pussy was outlined with a thin line of hair, enough to emphasize what lay between. The redhead, when she presented her cunt to Burnham, as he was undoing the lock that imprisoned her loins, leaned over and brushed his face with her stiff nipples. When he reached out to embrace her, she twisted away and joined her fellow dancers.

Finally, all of the five dancers had received liberation from the overwhelmed American. They were back on the stage rotating their hips, stroking the gap between their freed nether lips, peering back at the honored guest with languid, lascivious looks.

The music changed again and the women began to slowly circle the stage. The blond who had first presented her loins to Burnham, after the second pass, fell to her knees and then let her body melt to the floor. On the next pass, one of the brunettes, a saucy looking girl, fell gracefully down next to her and placed her face between the outstretched legs of the blonde. She rolled onto her side, her lips drinking at the fountain of the blond girl's crevasse, while the next girl joined her on the floor and pressed her lips to the brunette's quim. When all of the girls had descended to the floor, they formed a ring around the stage, all connected pussy to mouth.

The music lowered and the light dimmed. While the barely audible notes floated through the room, the females continued their oral ministrations to each other's hot, moist cunts. A large mirror was slowly lowered from the ceiling and fixed at an angle that the diners could see from above, the circle of young, beautiful women energetically supping at each other's distended holes. On the floor of the stage, outlined by the writhing bodies of the lovely women was an imprint of the rose tattoo that graced their bellies.

The moans of the excited women soon threatened to drown out the lowly playing music. Fakery by slaves was severely punished and the passionate moans of the women were quite authentic. Their nipples grew hard, their chests became flush. Their hips ground into the lips that caressed them. Demonstrating an exquisite control over their passions, they all started to moan with incipient orgasm at the same time. The blonde was the first to begin to shudder and groan, her lust having overflowed into an explosive orgasm. The brunette whose tongue lay deep inside her was next, and she writhed and jerked as her cunt's spasms tore through her. The young woman between her thighs was next and so on, until the cup of passion had been passed along the orgasmic circle.

When the women's bodies came to rest, their passions having played their course, the light on the stage slowly dimmed until the room was cast in darkness. Jake fingered the nine millimeter inside his jacket, tensing at his boss's vulnerability. When the lights arose, the women were all kneeling on the stage, their foreheads touching the floor, their wrists crossed behind their backs.

The diner party broke into enthusiastic applause. This was the signal for the five women to rise from their knees and scurry to the table, insinuating their heads underneath and between the thighs of the principal diners. Burnham's eyes were wild with lust as the blonde who had led the women in their Sapphic display began to unbuckle his pants and lowered his fly. When Burnham's eyes floated back and his face relaxed, Jake took it as his signal to temporarily exit the room and go for a smoke. The grizzled man at the other end followed suit.

Two hours later Jake and Burnham were returning to their safehouse. They were sitting in the back of the Lincoln and Tucker was driving.

"I don't get it Jake," Burnham said.

"What don't you get?" Jake replied.

I mean we met for four hours, ate like pigs, drank a shitload of vodka, watched those dancing girls fuck themselves wild and we got nothing done! I thought that we were going to talk business!"

"Things don't work that way here, Mr. Burnham," Jake told him.

"Then how do they work, Jake," the irritated tycoon asked him.

"Well, you know the very dark guy that sat on the other end of the table from me?"

"Yeah," Burnham replied.

"He's the, lets say, 'spokesman', for the 'Commission'.

"And so?" Burnham asked impatiently.

"So, he and I went out for a smoke. You may not remember it. You had the blonde dancer in your lap and I believe your cock was in her quim."

"Never mind where my cock was, Jake, get to the point."

"The point is that you can have just about everything you wanted. It'll cost you $3 million up front, 5% of the contract price you get on the pipeline project and some stepped up operations in the States."

"What?" Burnham asked, incredulous. "How do you know all of this?"

"I told you, I talked to the guy."

"He told you all that?" Burnham inquired impatiently, his voice peaking, near to shrillness.

"Yes," Jake replied quietly. "And he told me that you can have the villa you wanted, it's all picked out. It's about 250 miles northwest of here. The prior resident was selected for a Kalikastan 'reduction in force'."

"You mean he was laid off? How can that be?"

"Do I have to spell it out for you, Mr. Burnham? He's wearing cement galoshes, sleeping with the fishes, taking a long dirt nap. Get my drift?"

Burnham paled a little. "Okay, and…?" he asked, a little taken back.

"So his estate was forfeit. Lock, stock and barrel. You'll get the house and the fields, his house slaves, the workers who are under contract, the mansion and, what's more important, his ponygirl facilities."

"Christ, Jake, you did it!" Burnham exclaimed, happily patting the slight, reserved 'fixer' on the shoulder.

"They said that you can have the helicopter, but just to fly to and from the airport along a designated corridor. The cash has to be paid right away. You'll be awarded the construction contract in about a week. Import and export issues regarding 'supplementary' products, meaning the technology transfers they're looking for and the moving of other local products into the West will be done separately."

"Sounds good, Jake. You did a great job."

"Are you sure, Mr. Burnham?   Frankly, when I proposed this plan I thought that we would be sort of in and out. But these commitments are long term. And welshing would be a major problem."

"I'm not going to welsh on anything, Jake," Burnham remonstrated. "I always keep my promises."

"Just don't let your self get carried away with all the pussy, that's all. I was willing to get into this business with the girls to get the job done. But I'm not staying on as your security after that, and as far as I'm concerned, when we get your niece back, the operations in the States shut down. I'm not going an inch further with that than I have to."

"Don't worry, Jake," Burnham told him. "It'll all be taken care of."

"But what about the expansion of our operations in the States? How do we pull that off?" Jake asked.

"We'll just have to increase efforts, that's all," Burnham replied curtly. "I've talked to your business manager, Felix something. I'm opening a branch in Cincinnati. That'll expand our reach almost all the way to the west coast. Pickups in places west can overnight there."

"What?" Jake asked incredulously.

"You heard me. This thing is going to work."

"And what do you think that your niece will say when she knows that you enslaved hundreds of innocent girls just to get her free? Do you think that's what she would want?"

Burnham looked at Jake coldly, as the Lincoln swung through the gate of their *pied a terre*. "She'll be happy to be free, Jake. And I'll be happy that she's free."

"And all the other girls?" Jake asked. "And what happened to that girl at the farm in Georgia? The girl Maureen? My man Irving has called me twenty times looking for an answer. He's an important part of my team and we may need his help here yet. What did you do with her, Mr. Burnham? What am I supposed to tell Irving who I gave my word that she would be taken care of? Is she dead, or was she sold to some whorehouse somewhere to offset your expenses?"

"Now who's acting naïve, Jake? This was your plan. Are you having moral qualms now? You've already sent over thirty or so girls to be enslaved here. What about them? Is it the number of girls that bothers you Jake? Let me tell you that as long as you're willing to go along with selling even one of them to these bastards, you're in. So it doesn't make a difference whether it's one or one thousand. The principle's the same. You're in Jake, and you're in with both feet."

Jake realized the truth of what the multimillionaire was saying. He was in for a penny, in for a pound. Was he losing his soul or had he lost it already?

* * * * * * * * * * * * * *

The night before her first race, Maddy couldn't sleep. She and Persephone were lying on thick cotton pallets underneath Vadym's trailer. They were allowed to sleep next to each other and Maddy was comforted by the presence of her partner by her side. She could hear Persephone's regular breathing and tried to match her own to it to bring on drowsiness. But she was just too nervous to sleep.

She had been shocked at the crowd of people who come to see the pageantry of the pony parade. She could not imagine what it would be like on the actual race day. The eyes of hundreds of people would be on her naked form. She would be performing for their amusement like some kind of animal. Their roars of delight as the ponies passed by the grand stand earlier that night had curdled her blood. It was as if she had been transported back into ancient Roman times, when only the wealthy and powerful had rights and slaves were treated as a species less than human. She imagined what the people who had been fed to the lions must have felt like, a piteous spectacle for the amusement of the masses. And while she did not expect to be eaten tomorrow, she did fear the consequences of losing.

It had been an almost idyllic time during her training with her new driver. She had learned his name, Vadym, more than she had ever known of her original trainer. He had whipped them only once, and that was when they had failed miserably to learn proper starting technique. Other than that, he had been kindly to them, stroking them affectionately, giving them twice daily oral release.

And the slave girl, her tender hands and loving glances made Maddy feel warm and cared for. Vadym seemed to have affection for the diminutive blonde, since she never saw him treating her cruelly, and every night she could hear the sounds of them copulating above her in the trailer. While Maddy had never heard her talk, she had heard her moan and cry out in pleasure almost nightly.

There was so little that she knew of what went on around her. Was tomorrow's race the point of all of her training, or would there be other races? How long would she be able to have the blond pony by her side? How soon would she be returned to the mercies of her master, the one who trained her? When would the cruel owner of her flesh take his due? Would they be punished if they lost tomorrow?

The ponygirl tried to imagine what she and her sister ponies had looked like as they pranced in honor of their lords and masters. She saw in her mind their naked flesh, their bare breasts bobbing and shaking, their nether lips wide open for all to see. And their hoods, what was it like to see a stream of human females, all melded into one identical set of facial features, a bump for a nose, lips spread in a fierce grimace as they accommodated the devilish bits in their mouths?

And what about the ponies she would run against? How long had they been ponies? Were they more experienced? Faster? Better trained?

Maddy heard the slave girl through the wall give a prolonged moan of pleasure. Her own pussy longed to be filled by her driver's prick. On those nights when it was her turn to suck him off, she would imagine the thick instrument that was in her mouth plowing her hot, moist slit. But her crevasse would lay open and empty like a chasm, and she would need to wait for the delicate fingers of the slave girl to give her release.

She did not know how long she had lain there awake, but she ultimately found herself waking to the gentle nudges of the slave girl. The girl pulled up the flaps on her hood, freeing Maddy's eyes, and unshackled her ankles and collar from the stakes that had been pounded into the ground. She and Persephone had a quick breakfast and took their turns being groomed by the petit blond. When done, they were tethered to the back of the trailer by the rings in their noses and they waited.

Vadym came down from the big house about a half hour later. He was walking with a small group of drivers and chuckling at some joke that had been made. His face seemed cheery and relaxed. When he approached the trailer, he stopped to caress the hindquarters of his racing ponies. He slipped his hands between their legs from behind and began to stroke their sexes. Maddy spread her legs dutifully to receive her driver's caress. It was not long before her breath started to shorten and her crevasse began to dilate and warm. Vadym stopped when he sensed that their arousal had started to peak, and the ponies whined as his hands were withdrawn. The driver went in to don his informal riding clothes. The ponies would be taken out for a spin on the track, to keep them warm and reduce their tension. It would also help them get the 'feel' of the track that day, whether soft and difficult to gain traction in, or hard and compact, a dream for the fleet of foot.

Maddy did find it relaxing to be jogging around the track. The other ponies were doing the same and it was almost like a promenade. Each time as the team leisurely coasted through the home turn, she could catch a glance at the grandstands filling up. She wondered if the young Russian whore from the night before was there. Was she laughing and pointing Maddy out to her companions? Did she spread her legs last night for the handsome man who had accompanied her or whom she was accompanying? Did she sleep in a warm, comfortable bed last night and put on her own makeup this morning looking at her own face in the mirror?

At about eleven, she and Persephone were driven back to the trailer. The slave girl got them lunch and then cleaned and repolished their shiny pony cart. Vadym gave them both rubdowns, but instead of bringing them to climax with his skilled tongue and lips, he stopped a little past midway, leaving the moaning ponies to their unresolved passion.

About 12:30, Maddy began to see from her vantage point behind Vadym's trailer the various other pony teams being harnessed up. About twenty minutes later the first pony team, a four in hand chaise, came loping along the pathway to the track. Soon afterwards, she could hear the crowd cheer as the first ponies of the day began to warm up. And, about twenty minutes after that, she heard the flourish of trumpets, announcing the imminence of the first race. There was a shot and a large roar from the crowd. She could hear a man's voice calling the race over the loudspeaker. The voice's intensity grew as she imagined the ponies rounding the turns. In her mind's eye she saw them dashing down the home stretch. There was a momentary increase of decibels in the crowd noise and then silence. About fifteen minutes later, the four pony cart was pulled over the small hill that separated the campground from the track. The ponies were all wearing garlands around their necks and they were stepping proud and lively. She heard a round of applause run through the campsite.

Maddy listened to the races progress, standing tethered by her nose to the rear of the trailer. Twice, the slave girl had come around and teased her nether lips until she felt dilated and moist. Each time she stopped when she sensed that Maddy was ready to peak. Maddy whined with disappointment and the tension of unfulfilled lust was beginning to make her skittish. She watched as her partner suffered the same fate. After the third race, the slave girl began to put on their harnesses. Maddy's stomach was in a knot as the straps were pulled tight. Vadym emerged in his racing finery and began to massage her thighs and shoulders. He did the same for Persephone and the two ponies were hitched to the gleaming cart. The team pulled the cart to the top of the rise. Maddy could see the giant landau coaches being pulled around the track by their nine pony teams. The crowd was cheering them on as the announcer called the play. As she watched, the slave girl, who had come up to the rise with them, began to stroke her pussy lips once again. Maddy closed her eyes as her lust began to grow. She yearned for climax as the fingers tormented her. Her breath became deep and labored. All of a sudden, the hands were withdrawn. She felt a snap of her reins and she automatically started forwards.

Now she understood the tantalizing treatment she had been receiving. Her blood was up and her whole body tingled. Her legs felt electric as she trotted beside her equally stimulated partner towards the track. They reached it just as the red team did and they pulled out on the track together. Vadym had to hold their reins back to keep a restraint on their excitement.

The yearling races are considered by many a novelty item. The ponies really don't have that much training, and since they are teamed with another pony, the casual observer really can't see how much individual strength or stamina they have. But the cognoscenti can tell a lot by how a pony pulls at her reins, how steady and firm her posture is, how graceful and strong are her legs. More than one student of the sport noted Maddy's almost feverish struggle to restrain herself. Her team had been going off at three to one because of Maddy's limited training, but the smart money soon reduced it to 2 to 1.

Vadym led his team around the track twice at a medium pace. He wanted their legs nice and loose for the 1500 meter sprint. His ponies had never run an actual race, although he had paired them off a few times with some of the other teams just for the experience. He knew that they were anxious and he called out their names soothingly as they slowed down to address the starting line.

The starting line was a line of yellow chalk drawn across the track. The race would start in the back stretch and go one and a half times around, ending in front of the reviewing box. The crowd would twice get to see the graceful, naked yearlings straining mightily to maintain a torrid pace.

Maddy tried to put away her consciousness of her nakedness in front of all of these people. It was the first time that she was glad that she was hooded. Somehow having her face protected from view moderated her humiliation. Vadym kept the ponies' reins tight so that they would not be spooked by looking into the raucous crowd. The two teams stood next to each other ready to pounce at the sound of the gun. Maddy worried anxiously that somehow her lack of experience would hurt them in the race. It might have been better to tell Maddy and her teammate that the other ponies were new too, and that they were also engaged in their first actual contest, but oral communications to ponies is frowned upon.

The reds had the inside pole. This meant that Vadym's team would have just that much longer of a race. But the trick was to fight for the lead and make the other team take the long route around.

Vadym tugged the reins gently to get the ponies' attention. The crowd silenced as the race was about to begin. There were about six or seven tortuous seconds and then the gun exploded.

Vadym's team jumped to an early lead. Their incessant training at the starting line was paying off.

The 1500 is just long enough that two ponies lugging a carriage and a man, light as he was, cannot take the whole race in a sprint. There is strategy, just like in any other sport. Vadym took advantage of their early lead to gain the inside track. He kept them there until just after passing the reviewing stand for the first time. He knew the driver of the other rig well. He liked to get his ponies out fast and run the other team's legs off. But Vadym knew that Maddy's endurance had not yet fully caught up to her speed and he wanted a slower first third of the race. Using the ponies' trigger like response to the slightest pull on the reins, he had been gently edging the team to the right each time that the red team began to make a run at passing them. Blocking was strictly prohibited, but an experienced driver could let the drift of his team make the passing team work twice as hard. When they reached the first turn for the second time, he let the red team pass.

Maddy was frantic to see the red team pull ahead. She yearned to break out into a full sprint, but Vadym was holding her and Persephone back. Her thighs were pumping furiously and the sweat was running off of her in rivulets. Her heart was pounding heavily in her chest. She knew that she had more than she was giving her driver and desperately wanted to throw off her traces and catch the reds. But she was a well trained pony. She had had it drummed into her a thousand times not to think or anticipate, but to obey the messages that she felt passed on to her through the reins by her driver. All that running blindfolded had curbed her willfulness. If Vadym hadn't tugged the reign a little to the left at the turns, she and Persephone would have run right into the guard rail.

The two teams were midway through the backfield. Maddy could not hear anything above the roar of her own blood in her ears. Drabik, sitting on the edge of his seat in the grandstand, watched his protégé dashing down the long stretch. His blood was hot too as he yearned for her victory. "Come on, come on, you old fool," he thought to himself, "Let them run, let them run. Do it now!"

As if he had read Drabik's mind, Vadym gave the reins a mighty flip and the two blue and gold capped ponies leapt into life. He steered them carefully, wasting not an inch of track, until they cleared the red carriage's right wheel. He snapped the reins, jerking the ponies' heads up, signaling a full sprint.

Maddy was thrilled to have been given her head at last. She knew from experience that she would have to keep in time with the slower Persephone, but she had been able to draw the best out of her yellow tailed partner before and she knew that she would drop dead in her harness before she would let Maddy down.

The two teams rushed madly around the near turn and headed into the home stretch. The crowd had gone wild, having expected a typical blasé effort from two neophyte teams. But Vadym had made a race of it and his ponies were slowly gaining the edge. Maddy could hear the high pitched grunts and groans of the females of the red team as she and Persephone pulled abreast of them. Her legs pounded into the turf, toe first, straining for every ounce of strength and speed. "This is what I am," she thought to herself as she drew out every ounce of effort. "I am a pony, a fast pony, a winning pony! Run! Run! Run!" she commanded herself.

A hundred yards, seventy, sixty. At thirty yards, the red team, who was still ahead of the blue and gold by a nose, seemed to give out. Their driver had over estimated their abilities by thirty yards. Maddy and Persephone were still pounding away madly at the turf. Maddy sensed the finish line ahead of her. She sensed having gained the lead. Her lungs bursting, her legs throbbing, her heart pounding, she dug down and found that last bit of needed energy to pull herself and Persephone across the line.

The crowd went wild. There was cheering and chanting and rhythmic clapping as the teams took a turn once more around the track to cool off their tortured muscles. Maddy strained hard to regain her breath. Her breasts were heaving and her blood was pounding in her ears. Had they won? What had happened? Her sight was restricted to straight ahead and so she wasn't sure.

She and her pony partner were full of anxiety as they trotted slowly around the clubhouse turn. The crowd was still earnestly cheering and chanting. As they approached the reviewing box, the red team pulled up next to them. Vadym pulled his ponies to a halt and he leaned over to shake the hand of the other driver. And then, as the red team began the long trek back to their campsite and whatever fate awaited their failure, Maddy and Persephone were pulled into the winner's circle. A small crowd surrounded them. Grobgy was there, beaming at the success of his yearling team. Vadym was the master, he thought. And how the auburn haired one had run! Drabik had been right about her. He caressed Maddy's breasts as he stood before the two pony team. He then turned to Persephone and repeated his gesture of ownership. Anya was there too, vowing terrible tortures on the cunt of Drabik's fucktoy. Maddy was too excited at the fact of having won her first race to take note of anything but the excited people around her. Vadym was handed a bouquet of bright flowers and garlands were placed around Maddy's and Persephone's necks.

As her euphoria died down, Maddy became aware of her total nakedness before the finely dressed throng around her. She remembered that to these people, she was a faceless beast. She began to paw the ground in front of her nervously. Persephone apparently, too, felt the incongruity of being a hooded, naked female among this crowd of real people. She shifted her stance in the traces and pulled her head side to side.

Sensing his ponies' dismay, Vadym waved off the celebrants and began to back his rig up by a skillful manipulation of the ponies' reins. It was a maneuver they had practiced, and the rig slowly edged out of the crowd. When he felt that he had enough room, Vadym wheeled the ponies to the right and took them back out on the track for the trot home. The crowd was still excited, however, and he decided to give his ponies a little thrill. Instead of turning off and towards the campgrounds, he maintained their pace on the track for a victory lap. Seeing the ponies trotting energetically once more around the dirt loop, the crowd began to chant and cheer again. When they passed the reviewing box, he had them break into a cantor, legs high, bodies back. There was a final cheer from the crowd and then he took the ponies home.

Maddy felt a surge of pride as the team crested the little hill and heard the applause of the other drivers and handlers in the camp. The slave girl ran out to grab their reins, her eyes alight. When the cart came to a halt, Vadym jumped off and, smiling broadly, patted the heads of his victorious ponies. They were unhitched, their bits exchanged for the less burdensome gags, and led into the shielded area of their campsite where their rubdown table was waiting. Vadym hoisted Persephone up first, and Maddy watched as he laid his hands on her, rubbing the tired muscles. She waited expectantly, as he tongued Persephone into ecstatic pleasure.

Maddy's pussy was already wet as Vadym lifted her up and placed her face down on the table. His hands were hot and her skin electrified wherever they roamed. When he rolled her onto her back, her legs spread eagerly, anticipating the pleasure of her driver's skilled tongue and lips. He did not disappoint. She felt his tongue trace the lines of her labia, his lips suck in the nub of pleasure at their peak. She moaned as he drove her passions higher and higher. In the background she could hear the crowd roar as the next race went off, the 1500 sulky. She reexperienced the thrill of her victory as Vadym's tongue darted deep between her cunt's folds, tickling the special spot at the roof of her hot canal. He flicked the tip of his tongue repeatedly against her hard clit and sent wave after wave of intense pleasure coursing through her. When she came, she groaned with delight, her thighs quivering, her heels digging firmly into the table.

The slave girl showered the two ponies and led them to posts that had been set in the ground by the pathway at the rear of their trailer. They had been given fresh, clean hoods and the garlands had been restored around their necks. Maddy felt the rear ring of her collar attached to the top of the post and her ankles affixed to two rings that had been pounded into the earth. She and Persephone stood there displayed as the last racer topped the hill wearing her own garland of victory.

It had been a banner day and when the racing was over, the trainers and other pony workers who had been watching the races flowed into the camp to help celebrate the victory. Hands patted the ponygirls' heads and caressed them between their nether lips as happy faces peered into their small eye holes and voices issued congratulatory phrases. Maddy felt untold lips kiss her taut nipples as hands excited her loins. After a short while, she was afire with lust. She came three times during that afternoon, her knees almost buckling as her pussy throbbed with pleasure.

When she saw the hard, cruel face of her trainer looking at her, Maddy's heart quailed. He looked at her sullenly, his eyes displaying a morbid intent. He grabbed her tender lower lips between his fingers and pressed them hard together. His message was clear. Today may be a victory and Maddy might be the belle of the ball, but sooner or later, she would back in his domain and under his power.

Drabik left quickly and the rest of the afternoon was spent enjoying the attentions of the pony staff. After two hours, the slave girl came to release them. They were fed and each given a chocolate as celebration of their triumph. When their gags were restored, they were permitted to sit on the bright blue and gold blanket together. The two ponies were sitting cross legged on the blanket, their hooded heads leaning together in mutual friendship, when Maddy felt the presence of an intruder in their little island of peace. She looked up and saw her owner, the tall, dark mustachioed man, standing over her. She gave a start and she felt a tremor of fear in her stomach. He snapped his fingers and both ponies leapt to their knees.

Grobgy had come to inspect his victorious property. Vadym had been in the caravan and when he stepped out, happy words were exchanged between the two men. Vadym handed the bandit chieftain a tumbler of vodka and they toasted each other. The driver then withdrew to his comfortable chair. Grobgy turned to his prized yearlings and began to unbutton his fly. He stepped behind Maddy and pushed her over so that her head was on the ground. She felt his rough hands caress her hindquarters as he knelt down behind her.

It had been more than ten days since anyone had entered her body other than her driver, Vadym, and he had only used her mouth, permitting her to express her devotion to him on her knees between his legs. She had thought the blue and gold paneled wall of cloth around the trailer a sort of barrier to the world outside of Vadym's little family. She was upset to feel her driver's eyes burn into her as she exposed her rearward entrances to her owner.

Grobgy's hands encircled her breasts, which lay underneath her, squeezing them tightly as he rubbed his hardening cock along the valley between her rear cheeks. Her pussy had yearned for the presence of a hard cock, but she had not wanted this. She sensed the presence of her teammate kneeling stiff and upright beside her, too afraid to move, and she was ashamed when Grobgy's hand ran between her legs from behind and, stroking the gap between her lower lips, drew a moan from her.

Maddy felt Grobgy's stiff pole demand entrance at the gate to her womb. Its thickness spread her labia and expanded the walls of her moist slit. Maddy clenched her eyes shut in shame as the cock drew slowly across her hardened bud and, at the same time, groaned with pleasure. Despite her unhappiness at being used so callously in front of her trainer and the others, her lust rose with each thrust of the hard cock. Grobgy shoved himself deeply into Maddy's tight tunnel and then slowly withdrew until the bulbous head lay just inside. He then pressed forward gradually and deliberately until he was again sunk to the hilt inside her.

The ponygirl chewed at her gag in agonized frustration as her owner's cock pushed her lust higher and higher. Her orgasm hit her all at once, and her pussy gripped Grobgy's member tightly. She heard him laugh and call out something to Vadym, who laughed back. She could not prevent herself from moaning and crying out as her pussy's hard contractions sent jolts of pleasure through her. She cursed herself for a fool as her utter helplessness was brought home to her anew. Moments ago she was reveling in her success. Now she was being reminded of her bestial nature, a subhuman female, whose wants, feelings and desires meant nothing.

When her spasms subsided, Maddy felt Grobgy's prick withdraw from her hot, wet cunt. She whined with misery as she felt it pressed to her smaller hole. With her lubrication on his cock, Grobgy was able to gain access to Maddy's bowels with ease. Her anus tingled with pleasure as his cock rasped against it. Almost immediately, her hunger for fulfillment rose again. She felt filled by her owner's meat and her slit began to tingle and throb with her expectant lust. Her mind now cleared of any thoughts other than the rigid pole that dragged across the tender flesh of her rear entrance. "Ohhhhhhh! Ohhhhhhh!" she moaned as the merciless cock pushed her closer and closer to another explosive orgasm. Suddenly, she felt the man behind her stiffen and heard him groan. His hot sperm jetted inside her and triggered in her a paroxysm of pleasure.

"Oh! Oh! Oh!" she cried behind her gag as she was overwhelmed with the waves of ecstasy that flowed through her. "Ohhhhhhhhh!" she cried again as Grobgy drew every last ounce of pleasure from her body.

When Maddy's owner and lord withdrew from her, he stood over her contemplating her sleek form. He had been neglectful in failing to appreciate the value of this former human female. He would come again to use her and when the season was over, he would direct his full attention to her.

Maddy listened as her passion ebbed while Grobgy laughed and exchanged pleasantries with Vadym. Was this the start of a new phase of her debasement, she wondered unhappily. How easily her owner had smashed her false idyll, the illusion of safety that Vadym's kind treatment had given her. She had somehow forgotten that his use of her was as dehumanizing as any of the others. To him, she was no more than useful beast, to be coddled or abused, as the situation determined.

But she had won a race. That must mean something. And she understood that her fate was very much tied in to her success as a ponygirl. That without that, she was nothing to these men. She would succeed, she promised herself as she looked down at the blue blanket beneath her, still crouched on her knees. If she was condemned to a servile existence and had lost all of her that was human, then she would strive to maintain her value to these depraved, cruel men as a swift, strong pony, as long as and as best as she could. Success as a pony meant pleasure;failure meant pain.

* * * * * * * * * * * * *

Jake took a long look at the vast property that was now his boss's estate. There was a huge, turreted Russian style dacha set along a copse of woods. There was a large dirt track for running the ponygirls. A large pony barn sat near the track, although it was mostly empty as the stock had been depleted by the depredations of the overlords of this gangster run nation who had taken advantage of the prior owner's demise.

But that was all mere cover, or was supposed to be, for his search for the kidnapped girl, Madeline Burnham. It would be like looking for a needle in a haystack, with 30 or more large estates with significant pony herds, another hundred or so other smaller barons of crime, licensed to possess and/or train them. And then there were the whorehouses too. Perhaps Maddy had been spirited off to one of them, assuming she had been deemed unfit to wear an owner's racing colors. Feeney, just before he was ordered to his knees to receive a bullet to his head, had told Jake that Maddy had been recruited for the purposes of being converted to a ponygirl, that she had been kidnapped based on specs sent out by one of the many ponygirl racers. He did not know who. Jake had been unable to wheedle out of Khalid any information about slaves that had passed through his domain. And when you could see only the naked bodies of the enslaved female ponies and not their faces, it would be nigh on impossible to single out the one who was Maddy. But he would try. Tomorrow, he would begin the search in the guise of filling his boss's pony barn. He would travel to the many estates that were marketing ponies, go to their races, do whatever had to be done. He had taken a contract to find and rescue Maddy Burnham, and he would not give up, regardless of how jaded his employer would become.